T0194360

Ramon's World

Beyond the Edge of Reality

POETSENVY

Order this book online at www.trafford.com
or email orders@trafford.com

Most Trafford titles are also available at major online book retailers.

Print information available on the last page.

ISBN: 978-1-4907-6597-6 (sc)
ISBN: 978-1-4907-6599-0 (hc)
ISBN: 978-1-4907-6598-3 (e)

Library of Congress Control Number: 2016900620

Trafford rev. 01/11/2016

www.trafford.com
North America & international
toll-free: 1 888 232 4444 (USA & Canada)
fax: 812 355 4082

The sun rose slowly over the horizon, sprinkling light across the pole beans and the corn. It was a peaceful scene but it was quiet only for the moment. Two men crouched in the shadows at the edge of the garden. They watched her gather radishes and onions and place them neatly in her basket.

They made no sound as they rose and stretched. They glanced quickly at the old dog lying beside her, and then in the other direction to see if there were others up and about. One of the men, in his thirties and the taller of the two, moved stealthily and eagerly towards her, excited that she was alone and unprotected. The man knocked the basket from her hands and stuffed a cloth into her mouth. He warned her, "Don't try anything, little girl. And if you continue to struggle I'll break your neck."

The second man, in his twenties and apparently the tall man's helper, looked for the dog but the dog had disappeared. He put his knife back into its leather sheath. If the dog showed up he would dispatch it quickly.

The tall man threw the girl over his shoulder and started towards the garden gate. He did not see a boy drop from a tree in the nearby orchard, slip the sack of peaches off his shoulder, and start towards them. But both men saw him slide over the back fence and stop between two bee hives.

Worker bees in both hive entrances were enjoying the sun's early rays, their wings stirring the air around the hives. The boy slapped his hand on one hive and then the other. "Wake up, queens! Wake up worker bees! I need your help!"

Irritated because he disturbed them, a few bees lifted and dove at him but did not sting. "They've got my sister and they're taking her somewhere!" The strain in his voice was evident. "Hurry!"

The boy was making too much noise. The men had not expected opposition. Their boss had assured them that no one would be watching and the girl could be captured. This boy was being a nuisance.

The taller man, his face angry and contorted, turned towards the boy. "O.k., little boy. Now I'll have to kill you and the girl."

His words were still echoing when a small tornado of angry bees left the hives, drifting towards him. One bee left the group, dove and hit the man below his left eye. It clung just for a second, left its stinger embedded in his flesh, and tumbled to the ground, all in one smooth movement.

Below the man's eye a small pouch, the bee's stomach, continued to pump venom. He grabbed the stinger and pulled it out, forcing more venom into his skin. Chemicals left by the dying bee drew the next series of bees. They planted their stingers close together, one after another. His exposed skin was vulnerable and a perfect target.

He swatted at the angry bees as they circled, his frantic efforts drawing them in. They were infuriated by his jerky motions and increased their attack.

The man yelled, "Help! Help!" But he found out that was a mistake.

Two bees flew inside his mouth, stinging his tongue. He spit the bees out but now he was afraid to call for help.

He stumbled forward, his eyes swelling. By now his eyes were just slits in his swollen face. He stopped, reached for Ana's throat, but a new wave of bees landed and stung. Sacrificing their own lives, they pumped new venom into his skin before they flew a short distance away and died.

The man released his grip on Ana and staggered to the garden gate.

It was already too late. His airway had swollen shut, cutting off his air supply. He fell head first into the grass.

The second man dove into a nearby ditch full of muddy irrigation water. He submerged and surfaced a few seconds later. Bees dove at him, caught in his hair, and he submerged again.

The bees circled and waited, ready to attack, continuing to hear the boy's commands. When the boy was satisfied the man could not harm anyone he released the bees from their attack. The bees quieted down and returned to their hives. A few minutes later, the man crawled cautiously out of the ditch.

Several neighbors had noticed the excitement. They rushed over and gathered around the strangers. One was lifeless, the other man hysterical.

He pleaded for mercy, confessed to his role in the attack, and made many excuses. The neighbors listened and took notes regarding his involvement and his confession. In a few minutes a police car came and he was escorted into town.

The man was not held long. Lawyers came and asked him a few questions.

The man insisted they were innocently attacked. "We were walking down the road and we saw this garden. We thought about taking a few vegetables because we were hungry. We were attacked by bees before we had a chance to get any."

He was released without being charged.

The boy and the girl were ignored. They were too young to be considered credible witnesses.

"Not enough evidence to hold him," the sheriff said.

"Are you o.k.?" Ramon asked Ana.

Ana smiled at her brother. "Thanks, Ramon."

"No, Ana. Thank the spirits and the queen bees. They saved you."

Government officials came to the garden that week wanting to know the truth behind the bee attack. They did not believe Ramon's story about the bees helping him.

"Boy, those bees are killers. One of those men died. Tell the truth, now, and you can get back to your games."

Ramon repeated the story several times but the officials wouldn't listen. They could find no evidence anywhere of someone communicating with bees.

"We'll have to destroy these hives. They're too dangerous to have around. They're full of killer bees."

Yellow tape was wound around the hives and everyone was told to stay away.

That night, while everyone was sleeping, Ramon gathered about two pounds of bees from each hive and put them in wire boxes suitable for shipping. He put the queens in little cages and placed them inside the boxes. When he was satisfied the bees could be safely handled, his mother drove him to the post office. The following afternoon he mailed his package bees across the country to his cousin.

"Take care of my bees, cousin. I will repay you when I can."

When news of the bee attack reached Ramon's father the townsfolk tried to make things sound better. They told the truth. They said Ramon was by the bee hives when two men grabbed Ana. Ramon tried to make them release her. He was a hero for protecting her.

Ramon's father did not want to hear about Ramon doing good deeds. He stomped up to the garden and said, "Ramon, I told you not to call the spirits for help. Digging up the spirits causes problems in this modern world. You are grounded. You will not be allowed in the garden for two months for disobeying me."

Ramon's father would not listen to Ramon's explanation. He never would. That was the way it had always been and would always be. Ramon's life was always well ordered and the spirit world kept at bay, ready to help.

With his father's strict guidance and corrections Ramon's world grew increasingly tighter as he struggled to meet his father's expectations. But beneath the surface Ramon knew the other world was waiting to intervene. The spirits could be held back at times but they could not be crushed. Because both worlds were real in his life Ramon had to keep one world wrapped in the darkness of his mind.

It could never coexist with his father's world. If Ramon acknowledged the existence of the spirit world his father might lose control.

When Ramon was two his grandmother brought him his first real toy, a cuddly gray rabbit with floppy ears. His father was furious when he saw Ramon holding the rabbit. He glared at Ramon's grandmother and said, "Do not interfere with our lives! No bunny rabbits or teddy bears! We hate rabbits! Rabbits destroy gardens! And toys are for the weak! Ramon will be a man, not a girl! I want him to grow up without all the emotional handicaps. He will be a scientist like me."

Ramon's father was adamant that Ramon grow up in a real world. "My son will not have a life of ease or luxury. He is expected to help the world, not as an imaginary superhero, but as a real scientist improving the world's food supplies."

EXPECTATIONS

Ramon didn't remember exactly when he began keeping his journal. It was just a way of keeping track of his normal life. He wasn't perfect and he wanted to remind himself of all the mistakes he made. He hid the journal every day after recording the day's events. He wrote about his dad and mom, his siblings, his ancestors, and people who affected his life.

Sometimes he made up fantasy stories. Within these stories he could create characters who would listen to him. Those characters did not have high expectations of Ramon. He could tell them, "I'm mad at Julie. She told on me to the teacher just because I pulled her hair." Or he might say, "I put a frog in Maria's lunch bag. Why didn't she scream? She smiled at me."

In his stories his dad was very strict and insisted Ramon follow the rules. "Someday, Ramon, you will understand why you cannot play with your friends every day. You have to get ahead. This world is not for the idle ones. If you learn good work habits you will have an advantage. Do not argue. Do what you are told. Someday you will travel throughout the world and many famous people. That's how I met your mom. We discovered each other at the Fiesta of the Gardens".

Sometimes at night he couldn't sleep. He worried that his parents might find out how bad he was. Would his dad beat him or send him away to boarding school like he threatened? Would his mom quit loving him if she knew he teased the girls at school?

The journal kept the collection of all the things he remembered. Whenever possible, Ramon listed the details of everything he had done that day. His dad would not be happy if he knew Ramon did any bad things.

Someone was calling him. A voice was penetrating his thoughts. Usually he could ignore or shut out anyone except his father.

"Ramon, where are you? Aren't you going to join us? Tonight we're having blueberry-peach pie and vanilla ice cream. If you don't hurry it will be gone before you know it." His mother's voice sounded delicate and beautiful, like chimes singing in the wind. He knew she made the best pies of anybody in the world: homemade crust, lattice top, a crust that was flaky and light. He could picture the pie now and he licked his lips in anticipation.

This time of year excited Ramon. The orchard was filled with green fruit. Soon the fruit would display the rich colors of its kind: red for apples, purple for figs, and splashes of red and yellow for peaches. The vegetables in the garden were also growing rapidly. The tomatoes were above the wire cages waiting for hot days, the lettuce was growing sweet and tall, and the peppers were color coded according to their fiery intensity. Each day his aunts prepared delicious combinations of fruits and vegetables for him from his personal garden. He was spoiled and knew it.

"I'm coming, mama, just as soon as I finish this row."

Ramon loved working in the garden even when he was tired and sweating profusely, the weeds had stickers, and the ground was as hard as cement. He enjoyed planting the seeds of each kind of plant. He wanted to be first to identify the seedlings as they pushed their way into the world. If he demonstrated that he knew the good plants from the weeds, he was allowed to keep the weeds out of his assigned plot. Any new task that was added became part of his list of things to do. While other children were playing Ramon was working. He planned his own garden, prepared the ground, planted the vegetables, harvested the produce, and finally, cleared the land when the plants were non-producing and barren of fruit.

In the garden Ramon had freedom to experiment and he enjoyed that freedom. It was the only place his father left him alone.

There was no point in arguing with his father. It was always done his father's way, and his father was always right.

Ramon simply said, "Yes, Father," and that was that. His mother came to him later and said, "The spirits say you will always be welcome to call on them. They will notify all things, whether living or not, that you have their support and powers. Just be careful when you use the powers. Many people envy you."

His mother called again. "Ramon, we are waiting for you."

He felt stirrings inside and knew his ancestors were telling him to listen to his mother. He wanted to complete his task yet he knew he should join everyone before it got too late. He carried his hoe to the fence and left it. Tomorrow he would finish the section of the garden he agreed to do.

He stumbled over a big clod as he walked through the garden. He thought, "Is that a potato sticking out of the ground?" He stepped closer to it. "No it's just my imagination. I'm stumbling over things now. I'll chop that clod into smaller pieces tomorrow and get it out of my way.'

His mother said, "Go wash up. We've been waiting for you."

There were spirits within his dreams, in the trees, rocks, and animals around him. He felt them and heard them talking. His mother told him constantly he had the ancient powers of the Aztecs in his blood. He was royalty and the powers were carried in his genes. His mother was convincing when she said the spirits were ancestors sent to guide and protect their family in difficult situations.

Ramon loved his mother and believed her but he feared his father. His father did not want any conversations about the spirits in his home. Ramon and his older brotherf met severe punishment if they mentioned anything that was out of the ordinary unless it had a scientific explanation. Ramon's world would always be under a light, tested and proven. There would never be room for fantasy, especially if it was more real than the concrete world within his grasp.

Thus Ramon grew up in a world within a world. One he could imagine and test. The other world was hard to imagine and hard to test. But he knew both worlds were real and he could never completely sort out the truth.

STORYTELLING TIME

Aunts were there, gathered in a storytelling circle. He looked at them carefully. They looked very much alike. Their long black hair was almost the same length and they had dark expressive eyes. They were almost the same height and they were delighted when people were confused and called them the wrong names. "We can eat while we tell our stories," one of them said. "Gardens and stories should never be neglected."

Ramon had always been quiet, thoughtful, and responsible. His parents expected him to keep everything organized and neat, whether in his room or in his section of the garden. Sometimes he felt the pressure of being perfect and he carefully hid any mistakes and shortcomings from his parents. Would they still love him if they found out he was ordinary?

His aunts reminded him constantly that great things were expected from him. His older brother had been subjected to the scrutiny of his relatives and when his brother ran away and enlisted in the military it put all the attention on Ramon.

"Ramon, you are a prince and don't ever forget that. Long ago our tribe was selected by visitors from other worlds. Our clan was given special powers to connect with nature. It became part of our genetic make-up. Ramon, you are able to converse with our ancestors as well as with nature. Tonight we will show you how to use some of your powers. You will have the discretion to use your ability whenever you need to. You also have the responsibility to never abuse it doing frivolous things. If it is used wisely it is a gift that can help all mankind."

This was a moment he would always remember. In their eyes he was now mature and trusted. He would be given adult status as a story teller. As a child Ramon heard story after story about his ancestors and their encounters with gods who came to earth in the form of animals. His mother and aunts, well known for their knowledge of Mexico's history and details about their own ancestors, told these stories over and over as truths that should never be forgotten. As a result, Ramon knew the names and actions of all the animal characters as well as the names of related generations of hard-working farmers and ranchers. Ramon often heard the animals talking to him. "Ramon, be our friend. Play with us." But he did not dare to play when his father was around.

Whenever his mother or one of his aunts started a story a crowd would gather, all work would stop, and all was quiet until the story came to an end. Rosa, Ramon's oldest aunt, would begin with facts. "Listen my friends, long ago in the heart of Mexico the Aztecs created beautiful gardens in an area that was very difficult to farm. Their floating vegetable gardens, called chinampas, were artificial islands and very fertile. The Aztecs became master gardeners and were honored throughout the lands. We are made of the same blood and when we die our spirits will remain to guide the believers."

Ramon always listened respectfully, even when their stories deviated from stories the local priests and nuns had taught him. Yet both kinds of stories were similar and clear and emphasized several points. The priest said, "Listen, my son. Our ancestors loved the land and insisted that every living thing must be treated with respect. Whether crops were grown or animals were raised for food, a portion of the surplus was always shared with the poor. A part was used to replenish and restore the land. And finally, one part would be used for experimentation and improvement of both plants and animals.

The Aztecs believed that life was connected by blood. When an animal was sacrificed its blood would cause the gardens and fields to yield bountiful crops. But don't forget to also give thanks to God for his generosity to our people."

At night the quiet moments became boring. When it was time for the telling of stories, everyone was invited outside under the stars. They gathered by a fire between two gardens where everything seemed mysterious and exciting. In the darkness all the answers to the unknown were waiting to be exposed.

Imaginations were free to explore in the safety of the group. Both young and old were encouraged to present old stories or create new stories about other cultures and civilizations. The stories grew with each telling and the fame of certain storytellers spread throughout the land. Ramon learned to be well prepared in order to keep his reputation as a storyteller untarnished. His intention was to become the best ever.

When his aunts contributed their ideas, their stories about fierce painted warriors who battled creatures and monsters came alive. Ramon could picture the warriors as they attacked and overcame unearthly foes. The stories became even more entertaining as other relatives and neighbors told new stories of romance and heartache, warrior kings kidnapping princesses from distant lands and starting wars, and some told animal stories similar to those by B. Potter or Kipling. Many stories became so real in Ramon's dreams that during the daylight hours he expected to meet the characters.

However, many stories at night were scary and involved the garden. Other stories gave Ramon information. His mother said, "This very garden is where I met your father. He was a scientist from Spain looking for new ideas regarding gardens and plants. On his first night here he told stories about a man created from body parts and brought to life with jolts of electricity. He scared us because he made the story real. I invited him back the next night for dinner.

The garden was where Ramon and his relatives felt the strongest connections with their ancestors. Ramon could not ignore the chills that ran up and down his spine as looked around. He could imagine eyes watching him as he waited his turn to share his story. He would always give thanks to the spirits for protecting his kinfolks and for protecting him.

Ramon's favorite was "The Big Toe", a story told often by his grandmother and passed down to become part of their family's oral history. Often he would beg to hear the story until someone would give in and begin. "A young boy was digging up potatoes one evening. The sun had already sunk below the horizon and the moon was creeping up into the sky." The story continued with all the listeners mesmerized by its simplicity or complexity, all depending on the storyteller's skills. If the garden was described with realistic terms, Ramon was drawn into the story immediately, wondering why that toe was in the middle of a row and looking like a potato. Was it the toe of an ancestor? There were many questions that needed answers. Ramon vowed to tell his children that story often.

IMPORTANCE OF GARDENS

Some nights the family sat around the dinner table discussing the topics of the day. The first question would always include their garden. "Ramon, were you responsible today? Did you clean out the weeds from the north corner of the garden?" Ramon's father might ask. Then he would begin a long discussion about the proper ways to clear the weeds, the best way to water certain plants, and the best way to protect plants and skin against the blazing sun.

His mother talked about nutrients and benefits of certain herbs and vegetables. She always claimed, "Rose hip tea is very popular. People are healthier when they get vitamin C. and tea is known to clean your system." And always she insisted every herb was better fresh from her own garden.

The discussions were usually mild and informative but sometimes Ramon's parents argued about which kind of knowledge was best for Ramon. Usually they compromised and said it would be better if he was well rounded, tying ancient knowledge to present discoveries and future changes.

In high school Ramon felt he was being torn apart. His mother and father continually fought about gardens and Ramon's future. His ancestors filled his dreams but his father and the priest continued to tell him that he could help his people the most by obtaining a degree and getting a good job. "Our country needs to become modernized. We need to give up the old ways."

His mother urged him to be a farmer for different reasons. "It's in your blood, mi hijo. Green vines grow from your feet. You have always loved squeezing mud between your toes. Rabbits, squirrels, birds, and other creatures know your name. But most of all, your ancestors live in rocks, trees, and the soil. They will watch over you. You will have a 'green thumb'. Your plants will flourish and grow even beyond the garden boundaries you will build and reinforce. Every year your garden will grow bigger and sweeter than the year before. Everything you touch will be blessed."

Ramon's father did not agree. "My son, you are going to college and getting a degree. Your ancestors are out of touch with the modern world. Their magic doesn't work well anymore. You will become an agronomist. Your degree will be in Plant Science. You will learn to improve and enrich the soil, help our food become disease resistant, and change their genetic structures to give us hope for our future. You can love what you do, but don't forget that everything must be done in ordered steps and recorded. Always give precise details so experiments can be duplicated."

Your mother's ancestors can still help you. My country and your people need to become more efficient. The things you learn in college will help everyone and how you use your knowledge is very important. The garden must be taken seriously. The rows have to be organized and laid out to get the most production possible. You will discover new plants. Some will be inedible and others will be dangerous. Some new plants will open new horizons. Ramon, you will be one of the top scientists in the world. Your discoveries might save this overcrowded world!"

Secretly Ramon worried about changing the genetic structure of plants and animals. He felt it would be a violation of the codes of his ancestors. They believed there had to be a natural solution to problems somewhere, some place that had yet to be discovered. Ramon also felt he was overstepping his agreement with God. Where was his faith? Did he dare ignore this God he couldn't see?

His mother said quietly when her husband left the room, "Ramon, just follow your heart. Your ancestors will guide you as you help the poor and needy. Money and fame are not as important as some people think they are. In your dreams you will be given advice. Listen carefully and follow it. If you ignore their advice they might leave you and never return."

Ramon secretly tried to listen to anyone with gardening expertise. However, he found it was hard to mix the modern techniques with ancient techniques. One scientist told him, "If you find special ways to grow and irrigate squash, tomatoes, onions, and corn, you will save many lives. We will be very grateful." Another scientist said, "Any success you have might stop some wars. Our nations fight over gardens and food."

He invited the scientists to see his gardens but they were too busy to honor his request. After all, what did a young man have to offer?

Ramon dug rows with a hoe and planted potatoes and root crops by the light of the moon according to advice from his ancestors and the Farmer's Almanac. Then to help the plants grow he put compost around each plant and irrigated his garden with a drip system. "Better to be over-prepared than be slack with my duties."

Then as the last thing on his list, he prayed. He asked that all his doubts be forgiven, and the widows, the hungry and the poor be given mercy. He also asked for love and peace to spread across the continent. And finally, he prayed that any blood used in a sacrifice be used to bless all who loved or were learning to love.

Later, as Ramon organized his supplies for college, his father stopped to talk. His face was expressionless. "Ramon, I want you to do your very best. Leave your fantasies and stories behind. Forget that non-sense. There are no ancestor spirits or talking rabbits. You are in this world all alone. There is no God. Do what you do best. Raise a garden. Make money. Live life to the fullest. Life is too short. Make sure you accomplish something you're proud of."

When Ramon began college he was still unsure of what was expected of him. He almost wished he could fail. There was so much pressure he hurt inside. There was so much to do and think about.

He wanted to help his country and he had dreams of helping the poor establish gardens that would raise standards of living. But he was nagged by one thought. How could he please his father and also his mother?

In all the confusion and turmoil his grades dropped. The words of his ancestors filled his dreams and he learned to ignore the harsh threats of his father. He realized he could help no one if he failed. Gradually he fought his way up in the college standings determined to become number one on the Dean's List. In the meantime his studies of certain root crops brought rave reviews and recognition as an up and coming scientist.

During his vacation Ramon traveled to several countries searching for ways to improve plants and soil. New experiences and changes opened his eyes to new possibilities. He met a girl who dazzled him with her beauty and energy.

Elena was entirely different from the girls he had known before. She didn't care about his ancestry or his college ambitions. She wanted to be a model and hang out with the beautiful people. Ramon enjoyed being with her, not because she cared about him and not because she cared about anyone but herself. Ramon enjoyed writing about the simple things she talked about. Her world was not intense all the time.

It did not take long before they tired of each other. Ramon did not fit her requirements as a husband. He was brilliant but too common looking. She simply wanted someone to look like the perfect husband and keep her own dreams alive. When his plans took his attention away from her, she was upset and warned him.

"I need your attention. Forget about the dirt your ancestors protected. You'll never get anywhere as a farmer. Don't worry about your job. You can get another one. Daddy has lots of jobs like yours. If I ask him he will find one for you."

He loved her but their relationship was doomed from the beginning. He had dreams and goals that he could not give up. She had dreams of traveling and socializing with people with money. Their worlds were crashing into each other. Ramon wanted to help people in third world countries. He was disturbed by stories and pictures of people starving and he knew he could do something to help. His wife enjoyed an active social life and could not understand why Ramon wanted to work in those hot, smelly places where life was difficult.

In spite of their personal problems they began their family. A daughter, Yolanda, was born. She was very special to Ramon and they bonded at once. As a young child Yolanda was talkative and full of energy.

Yolanda went everywhere with Ramon, to the park, to church, to his work, and sometimes to the zoo.

Ramon was startled at first when she talked to trees and rocks. He felt her connections to nature. In the city parks Ramon noticed that flowers and other plants leaned towards her as she chattered. "Hello, Mr. Iris. And how are you, Miss Daisy?" Gradually he became accustomed to her conversations.

When they visited the zoo Ramon had to adjust once more. Every animal waited for her to pass by and wanted to talk to her. His daughter had inherited his mother's connections to the spirit world.

Ramon understood her conversations but rarely participated or use his own gifts to converse. He pretended to be a non-believer. His daughter became the path the ancestors had been searching for to rejoin the outside world. Ramon sighed. He realized he could not stop her from using her abilities. If the spirit world could not go through him they would go around him.

CUSTODY

Ramon and his wife lived lives going in different directions. Soon they were living apart. Elena had social events to attend and he had lectures and meetings. They rarely talked to each other and when they did, they had nothing in common.

When his marriage crumbled, Ramon fought for physical custody of his daughter despite the odds against him. The judge called him aside and wanted to know why Ramon wanted custody of his daughter.

"Sir, your Honor, she is my responsibility. I love my daughter and I also have the responsibility of keeping her for our family, our ancestors, and those from our future. She is connected to our hearts."

His wife's lawyer argued, "The mother is always the nurturing parent. A man should not have a young daughter at home. He cannot treat her like a mother can. My client is willing to give him visiting rights but already he has influenced the daughter by his interest in the spirit world. I suggest that because of her tender age she be given to her mother."

The magistrate nodded his head in agreement but before he could give his decision verbally, something strange happened. A rabbit leaped and jumped across the back of the court room. It stuck out its tongue. The judge could not ignore its antics.

"Bailiff, remove that animal!" the judge ordered.

"Which animal are you talking about?"

"The one in the back of the room. Don't you see it dancing?" The judge's face was red and sweaty. "Doesn't anybody see it?"

While the court was in confusion and the judge distracted by a rabbit, the papers were signed and delivered to Ramon's lawyer and to the opposing council.

Ramon's lawyer looked at the papers and said, "Ramon, you got what you asked for. You have custody of your daughter."

His ex-wife's lawyer complained, "Wait, Judge. These are filled out wrong. They give custody to the father instead of the mother."

Ramon's lawyer said, "Whose signature is on these papers? If you change the papers now, this incident will make you look very foolish, Judge. First you see a rabbit, then it disappears. Then you want to change your mind regarding custody. This could go all the way to the Appeals Court and make headline news!"

The judge called for a brief conference. "I want the two councils to meet me in the judge's chambers." After a brief discussion they returned. The judge promptly gave his decision. "I believe this child should be placed with the father. Case dismissed."

Ramon did not tell the judge he saw the rabbit. In Aztec stories the rabbit is often the trickster. The rabbit had drawn their attention away from the impending outcome long enough for the papers to be signed. Ramon didn't report what his daughter was saying during the confusion. "xipe Totec," she said several times.

"The god of agriculture was here and he tricked the judge into signing those papers," Ramon said quietly.

Ramon's journal took up more than one book. Ramon had already exchanged four books of notes and stories for four empty ones. His father took up much of each journal. Ramon wrote down each item that displeased his father. One journal was all about Ramon's his father's displeasure with Ramon's divorce. It had to be Ramon's fault. If Ramon would negotiate or give in everything would be fine.

His father did not think a man should raise children. "That's a woman's job," he continued to tell Ramon. "How are you going to accomplish your dreams? I wanted you to become famous."

Ramon, friends with one of the presidents, had agreed to visit South America and be part of a science panel to convince farmers to try new techniques. When the custody battle was scheduled Ramon said custody of Yolanda was more important than anything else in the world.

His dad agreed to take Ramon's place. There should not be any bad publicity regarding the science panel. "Ramon, your reputation is at stake."

That month Ramon's dad was killed in a plane crash high in the Andes. The cause of the crash was never determined but Ramon thought it might be connected to him.

In his journal Ramon wrote the following poem.

ROOTS

Late last night a storm blew through, shattering trees,
I listened for this was not a common breeze.
Roaring and howling it stretched out wide,
The wind threatened as I shook inside.
A tremendous crash, then all was quiet.
In the silence I felt the anguish of a mighty tree.
It lay uprooted, its heart exposed.
Roots stretched out east to west,
The tree had been challenged and failed the test.
My life is much like that tree,
But though uprooted with my heart exposed,
I'm still me.
From my brokenness I will begin,
Stronger than before, soaring with the wind.

Ramon already felt guilty because of the divorce. His dad's death drove him deep into depression. The only thing he knew to do was to work harder.

Gardens are meant for show
And the major attraction
Is the satisfaction
Written on each grower's face.
Each girl or boy who tries to place
Values on growing his own,
Will find values fit for a throne.

Throughout his childhood and teens, Ramon's knowledge of plants and animals had astounded his teachers, friends, members of garden clubs, and even visiting scientists. Ramon seemed to have answers to every question about gardens, plants and animals. His expertise was noted and he was assigned a position answering questions on the internet and ran a column in a newspaper chain. When his answers were challenged he tactfully proved his knowledge. Not only did he remember the stories his mother and aunts had related about ancient gardens, plants, and animals, but his college training and field studies brought him acclaim as a reputable agronomist.

His reputation expanded as he conducted field studies in several countries. Although his work was improving the living conditions of the native populations he gradually withdrew from one country at a time. Earthquakes, tsunamis, hurricanes and typhoons, floods and droughts kept him busily solving natural problems, but he could not bear watching his countries fall into the hands of terrorists and tyrants while most of the world stood idly by, content to watch and ignore.

Many scientists were shocked when he said he would return to the states and accept an executive position in an agricultural firm.

"I can accomplish more if my work is kept safe and people are free to enjoy the fruits of my experiments."

His achievements were great but the poor were not protected in their own countries. Ramon dreamed of a world of peace, a world of fantasy where people cooperated with each other. He dreamed of quiet gardens of abundance. His father was right. Ramon had to work every moment if he wanted to fix his part of the world. Peace gardens had to be protected and fought for.

Yolanda, his daughter, was by his side as he traveled from one country to another. He thought he was being a responsible loving father by giving her directions and rules to follow. Ramon insisted she attend school and keep up with her formal studies. She listened and did as he asked but she felt as if her time was wasted. She knew her wisdom came from ancient sources but she was sure she understood plants and animals better than any of her teachers.

Out of his own past and feelings of guilt he expected her to be perfect. He knew he loved his daughter but he forgot to tell her and he forgot to spend his free time with her. Yolanda learned she had to rely on her own resources. Ramon knew he might be known someday as a great scientist but a terrible father.

She moved from school to school, learning bits and pieces of new languages. While Ramon worked with scientists and government leaders, Yolanda made friends in each town and each school. She attended the schools that were very poor and encouraged the students who were eager to learn.

Yolanda taught them how to grow gardens that produced enough vegetables for their own villages but also enough to sell at the outdoor markets. Whatever Ramon taught her about gardens, she passed that information to her classmates.

Because she taught with authority and knowledge wherever she went she was treated with respect. "Miss teacher", a girl would say, "the leaves on my tomatoes are yellow and dying. I water them twice every day. What am I doing wrong?"

Yolanda would say, "Maybe you're loving them too much. Talk to them but give them some freedom to grow. Only water them when they ask for water."

Ramon was caught up in the science of plants. He was discovering new varieties, new ways to help the plants grow faster, and ways for plants to grow in more hostile environments. His work consumed him.

YOLANDA

Yolanda heard about Ramon's success and she wished he could be there with her. She needed his strength and wisdom. Most of all, she needed his love and fatherly advice. Without her father she chose to be around older men who sounded wise.

In addition to helping in school, Yolanda had to constantly be on the alert for enemies who wanted to seize her for ransom. Although Yolanda was in danger, she felt her mission was more important than the fear of being captured. The political groups in some countries clashed violently and new leaders who sought control kept the countries in turmoil. Yolanda was not involved in any country's politics but she was important enough to be viewed as a target. She understood the risks but felt that the girls and women of each country needed education and freedom of choice.

Several times Yolanda escaped capture. Each time as opposing rebel forces came rushing in, she was already in the forest or jungle. Her animal friends warned her long before rebels got close. When a militant group burst into clearings or garden areas they were always disappointed to be a few steps behind. She became known as "the ghost" and "the spirit woman".

One evening her luck almost ran out. She was tired and ready to go to sleep. She was the last one up, writing entries in her log. Things were very quiet and everyone was either asleep or saying their prayers for the next day.

A few beds away a young girl was on a cell phone talking to someone. Yolanda, trying to be nice but wanting the girl to put her phone away, said, "You are new here and I know you must miss your parents. However, we must get our rest. The rules are very strict and all of us will be assigned extra chores if someone in our group violates the rules."

"Just a minute. They're almost here."

Yolanda asked quickly, "Who are you talking to?"

The girl ducked down into her blanket without responding.

"Everybody wake up!" Yolanda's voice rang with authority and the girls in her section stumbled into their clothes and stood waiting by their beds. "Girls, we are playing night games and we must wake the others without talking or making noise. We will follow the animals to our new hiding place."

The girl with the cell phone bounced out of bed. "Wait! I want to go with you. If I'm left I will be traded to a country far away."

> Two panthers suddenly appeared in the doorway. They growled and looked right at the girl. She took one step forward and the panthers moved one step closer. She lifted up her phone and threatened to call. "You move, Yolanda, and I'll call. You won't escape!"

Yolanda looked at the panthers and said quietly, "If this girl moves even one finger, eat her!" The panthers nodded and glared, their fangs dripping with saliva. "You know what to do next," Yolanda said as she raced out the door. She followed her animal friends into the jungle and led her group away from the school.

The girl with the phone stood frozen, afraid to move. The panthers had been joined by two more panthers and they all looked hungry. In the distance trucks and motorcycles were racing to get there. The other girls were waking up and were confused as the noise grew louder.

Yolanda returned and in a loud and clear voice she said, "Follow me and you will be safe. Stay and you will be killed or sold into slavery." There was little time to argue. The girls understood what the rebel forces could do. The girls wanted to hide in the gardens in the tall tomato plants but Yolanda insisted they would not be safe.

They followed Yolanda into the jungle. This time all were with her, even the girl who had been in contact with the rebels. The cell phone was no longer with the rebel girl. It was carried by a panther on a different trail going in another direction.

When the trucks and motorcycles roared into the camp the rebels were surprised by the quiet. No one was running around. No one was sleeping. They were angry their plan to surprise and capture the girls did not work. As the rebel soldiers checked each building they stopped and set a fire. Soon the entire compound was ablaze.

The blaze could be seen for miles. From their hiding place the girls could see the flames. The girls knew Yolanda had led them to safety, away from capture, torture, and even death. She urged them on even though they were sleepy and tired.

"When the sun smiles on us our enemies can also see. They will have cars and trucks, and my dears, they will have planes. We must travel fast and cross the border. Even then we will have enemies."

Yolanda knew the dangers and warned the other girls. Humans could be bought and sold, tortured and killed. The world ignored the atrocities that had occurred throughout civilization. Even the major world powers were reluctant to get involved in rescue operations. Truces might be broken. Most Civilized countries had their own problems. They pretended that slavery was over and the slavery trades were closed.

While Yolanda grew her own gardens with the help of her spiritual guides, all nature was attuned to her needs and safety. She was forewarned of any impending dangers and disappeared into the landscape. Her friends were not so lucky. Many were captured or killed. Yolanda was devastated when news of her friends came to her.

Political coups kept Ramon from living too long in any country. With all his knowledge about gardens and plants he could have helped so many people, so many nations, but there were always wars as people sought revenge, sought power and control, and wealth. Ramon tried to hide his disgust as his friends plotted against each other. He could read their feelings and understand their hearts long before they acted.

YOLANDA AND SERGIO

Ramon was oblivious to Yolanda's natural beauty and political value. But Yolanda was quietly growing up, full of wisdom and practical advice. Her beauty was admired by all except for her father. He still thought of her as his little girl. Therefore, when Yolanda appeared one evening with a young man in tow, Ramon was shocked.

The young man, Sergio, approached and boldly asked permission to talk to him. Ramon was enraged. The young man pleaded earnestly and reasoned with intensity and logic, pointing out Yolanda's loneliness and her need for a steady home life.

Ramon did not like the way Sergio treated Yolanda. Sergio demanded that she agree with him even when he was wrong. One day they came to visit and Ramon noticed Yolanda had a bruise on her face, her nose had been bloodied, and she was strangely quiet.

"What's wrong?" Ramon asked.

"It's nothing, Papa. I accidently bumped my head."

"How did you bump your head?"

"Papa, don't worry about it. It was my fault. I made a mistake, that's all."

Ramon suspected the worst but he listened to his daughter. If he knew for sure he would take action. Sometimes in his dreams his parents argued and he remembered a few times when the arguments ended with violence. His father would go out of control.

"Don't, Papa. Don't hit her." Ramon would scream. Often he would wake up in a cold sweat. He shivered and shook his head. Women should never be struck by a man.

His new son-in-law was arrogant and never admitted he made mistakes. When pressured, his anger flared and always someone else was blamed.

Yolanda loved him dearly and waited on him as if he was her king. Yolanda gathered fresh fruits and vegetables whenever she could and every meal was made especially for him. At first, Sergio complimented her on everything she did, but gradually he became more critical and controlling. He would sometimes fly into a rage when she did not have everything ready or if he didn't like the taste. "You expect me to eat this? You know I don't eat leftovers." Or "You made me late today. My clothes weren't ironed the way I like them."

Sergio isolated her with his disapproval and took away her contacts with friends and family. He berated her with questions. "Who did you talk to today? You don't have time to waste. Did you get your work done?"

Her friends made comments about how he treated her and gradually she withdrew from them. Ramon could see what was happening to her. She was once confident and very intelligent and now she was unsure of herself.

Ramon listened quietly when she talked about Sergio but he knew she did not want outside interference. "Papa, it's my life and I will do what I want."

JOSE

After Sergio and Yolanda were married three years, Jose was born. He weighed seven pounds and was nineteen inches long. From the moment he entered the world Jose was a quiet child. He didn't cry. He seemed alert to every sound, every new face, and every color. As a young child he smiled as he discovered new toys.

Jose had a very unique trait. He loved puzzles but he would not show any of his skills to strangers. Only Yolanda and Ramon were allowed to be his audience. If they were the only ones around he would take things apart and reassemble them. Ramon noticed that Jose would often draw the parts of a toy in exploded form. His understanding of directions made him very capable of handling challenges.

Sergio would have nothing to do with Jose. "Are you sure he's my son? My son would be talking and walking by now. Take him to the doctor and see what Jose's problems are. I don't want to see him until he's normal. He's a throwback to your ancestors."

Yolanda, was convinced Jose was brilliant, but doctors, nurses, teachers, friends and relatives would shake their heads and whisper that the child was special, but obviously brain damaged and traumatized at birth. If Ramon heard comments regarding his grandson he would usher the offending person out the door and say, "My grandson will be respected. Your words are hurtful and you have no evidence that something is wrong. Yolanda knows him better than anyone and I believe her."

Jose skipped the "terrible two's". It seemed life was too exciting for Jose to waste it being mad or crying. Each year as he grew older his personality did not change. He did not go through phases typical of most babies. He remained calm and happy and appeared to think about things without becoming frustrated. He had no siblings and therefore no competition.

In school he was the tallest in every class. His size was intimidating and the children at his school called him "Baby Huey" and made fun of him.

Most people treated Jose as if he was invisible. Since he never complained, they excluded him from conversations, chose teams without him, and ignored him whenever possible.

Jose chose the times he wanted to talk. He said what he wanted to say and meant for every word to have value. He had been curious about Ramon's journal and asked Ramon to help him get started. Jose was very careful to always put the journal in a safe place. He wrote his thoughts in a very concise manner. His private journal was never shared although he began talking to Ramon and Yolanda about students and teachers. Jose expressed his frustrations about being accepted and wanted to know why some students accepted him, but grown-ups didn't. Ramon did not explain that teachers were reluctant to waste their time on someone who could not communicate.

When he was in high school Jose still smiled in spite of how he was treated. He spoke little and refused to confront anyone except for certain reasons. He went by old rules, rules handed down from ancient times. No one was allowed to hit a girl. No one was allowed to bully or intimidate someone smaller. And no one could attack in groups.

Jose was tall and strong and very athletic. Those who challenged him were defeated easily and embarrassed. Jose did not boast or make derogatory comments and gradually his enemies became his friends and adopted his rules.

When Jose's counselor called, Yolanda thought, 'What's Jose done now? Has he finally lost his temper? Is he in trouble?'

Yolanda soon found out Jose was simply uncooperative. His teachers were very upset that he refused to talk about himself in front of classes. Yolanda called Ramon and said, "Your grandson is causing problems at school. Come and help me get things straightened out."

"The counselor wants to talk about Jose again. She says Jose won't succeed in college or in life unless he changes. He writes well but he doesn't want to read out loud or talk in class. He refuses to tell about himself or give short speeches. He cannot pass English unless he starts doing his required assignments."

"Is he causing other problems? Interrupting, or keeping others from learning?" Ramon couldn't understand the problem. "Is he failing mathematics or biology?"

"No, Papa. It's just in English and Spanish classes that he has this problem. He writes well and does well on written tests. He just doesn't like to talk out loud." She hesitated a moment. "Won't you go with me today to his conference? Maybe the counselor will listen to you."

Ramon looked at her thoughtfully. "You're his mother. If the counselor doesn't listen to you then why would she listen to me? I don't think being his grandfather gives me any special privileges."

"Yes, Papa, I know. But you have a job and respect. You're not just a farm worker. You're important."

That made Ramon angry. "There's nothing wrong with being a farm worker. My parents raised six children while picking oranges, grapes, and cherries. My brother and I finished college. All of us are good citizens and obey the laws. We respect the country we were born in and respect this country for the rights and opportunities it has given to us."

"O.K., Papa. That's why you should go to the conference. You speak out with passion. I get upset and worry about what I should have said and go away mad."

Reluctantly Ramon agreed to go with Yolanda. While he waited for the conference he reviewed the things he knew about Jose. Jose had never been a problem child. He worked hard at every job he was given.

He got along with others and completely his assigned tasks without complaining. His behavior was outstanding. How could anyone object to anything Jose did?

Jose frequently made one request. Perhaps his persistence was the problem. Many students listened to music as they worked. Could he listen to music? The music was barely noticeable and would not bother others. The rules about earphones were rarely enforced if students worked quietly. He only wanted to be treated like the others.

Yolanda told Ramon that Jose's request was always denied because teachers claimed he was behind in his work. If he gave his speech, his autobiography, he would be allowed all privileges the following semester. Everything seemed so simple and yet so complex.

Ramon stood by the kitchen window observing Jose. His grandson walked to their small orchard, glanced around, and then proceeded to an apricot tree. He reached up and pulled a small stool from the lower branches. He checked again to make sure he hadn't been followed and then reached up and brought down a second object. A book!

Ramon was puzzled by Jose's strange behavior. "What's this kid doing?" he mumbled.

Jose sat down, adjusted his glasses, and began reading.

'Perhaps,' Ramon thought, 'Jose is too shy to read in front of class.' Ramon couldn't hear the words but this time he knew Jose was practicing for an audience of some kind. Was the speech in English or was it in Spanish? It really didn't matter.

Jose stood up, took a few steps, bowed a few times, and then took pieces of lettuce and carrots from his coat. He scattered them in front of the stage. He sat down again and waited quietly.

Ramon was astonished as a few small rabbits and squirrels popped out of holes and moved toward Jose. Ramon murmured, "What's he doing?"

As he observed his excitement grew. "Wow! He's reading to them! I'll have to share this with his counselor. Jose does read to others. He's been hiding his ability to read from everyone, including me."

Because he was excited about what he had just seen, and because he was anxious to be punctual, Ramon left in a hurry and he did not see the mass of rabbits gathering by the imaginary stage nor did he see the squirrels pushing and shoving to get the best viewing spot possible.

Although they were making lots of noise, he could not hear the rumble when the rabbits thumped the ground in unison. The squirrels chattered and whistled loud enough to get the attention of tourists who had stopped for lunch.

The tourists pointed up the road as Ramon passed in his car. They shook their heads in bewilderment. Ramon thought they were talking about him. "Imagination plays funny tricks just before a storm," Ramon said as he entered the school's driveway.

Ramon would have enjoyed seeing the confidence in Jose's eyes as he opened his book. Ramon would have enjoyed the guitar even more. Instead of watching Jose with content Ramon was coming to school to protect his grandson. He had failed Yolanda in many ways and he was determined to give Jose a better chance.

The counselor thought her conference with Yolanda and Ramon would go smoothly. She was wrong. Ramon entered the room with fire in his eyes. "Why are you picking on my grandson?" he asked. "There are several discrepancies in the way my grandson has been handled. Jose has been treated like he's not very smart. The administration at this school has allowed the staff to bully him. "That will not be tolerated. If there are any instances of you or any of the other staff confronting him without due process this school will have more lawyers than students hanging out in every classroom. I'm not threatening you or anyone else but justice will be served. Do I make myself clear?"

The counselor looked shocked. "Would you like to speak to the principal?"

After Ramon and his lawyers met with the principal, the superintendent, and the school board, Ramon was given weekly written reports about Jose's status. Ramon insisted that Jose be transferred to a charter school within the district while a suit against the district was being considered.

There seemed to be little time to talk to Jose. Each of their lives was going faster than ever. Ramon was promoted to vice president of Statistics and Logistics fifteen hundred miles away and moved immediately. Jose was in a charter school. He was being challenged to reach his self-set goals. Both Ramon and Jose were in new situations with steep learning curves. They would have to get together later.

Although Ramon was living in Kansas City his job required him to travel throughout the country. He was on a business trip in California and intended to visit Yolanda and Jose as soon as he completed his business contacts. He wanted to check on Yolanda and see how her marriage was going and how Jose was doing in college. It was fortunate that he chose that day to visit.

Sergio was getting more abusive and violent. That day he came home looking for Yolanda. He was high on drugs and in a foul mood. Yolanda was in the garden picking vegetables for his dinner when he approached. She did not argue when Sergio said, "Yolanda, you've made my life miserable. You have not given me the opportunities I need. You have not used your abilities to help me crush my enemies. I could become King in many countries. With your help my empire would expand and thrive."

With the urging of the ancient spirits she spoke up. Although she didn't want a confrontation she said, "I don't think that's best for us. You don't have any plans to help the poor."

Sergio was enraged. He threw tomatoes and soft vegetables at first, smiling as the vegetables splashed across her clothes. Then he pelted her with potatoes and onions. "You will learn to be obedient. With training, mi esposa, you will be loyal and never disagree with me."

"Julio! Daniel!" he called out. Two muscular men came into the garden. They were confused at first by his order. "Take this woman to the compound! This woman will not be allowed to disobey me. Guard her closely. If she gets away, your lives are meaningless. Inform Sebastian he must begin training her at once. She will be made an example for others."

Daniel and Julio grabbed Yolanda before she could run. They wrapped duct tape around her hands and also tied her feet. Duct tape covered her mouth. The trunk opened and she was unceremoniously dropped in and everything went dark.

"I hate spiders," Yolanda mumbled. She woke from a deep sleep and found herself in a dire situation. She was not at home in bed, warm and dozing. Around her everything was dark, but she gradually noticed small pinpoints of light.

She tried to brush away a spider that was walking slowly across her face. She couldn't move. "What's going on?" she whispered to the face next to hers. He didn't answer.

'How rude,' she thought. 'This must be a really bad dream. Why can't I move?'

The spider was still there, trying to decide whether to enter her nose or her open mouth. Yolanda closed her mouth and gritted her teeth. There was nothing else she could do but wait and to see if the spider wanted in.

Voices were invading her dream. She listened carefully, trying to decipher their messages. Yolanda was irritated when they laughed about how easy she had been to fool. She wanted to protest but remembered the spider. She tried to move her hands again but realized they were tied.

The face next to hers remained frozen, the eyes open, the mouth closed. Death was waiting for her, too, but the spider had saved her for the moment.

Her senses were returning but she was still in a dream-like state. She thought she remembered sitting at a table in Sergio's favorite restaurant. He mentioned a robbery that had gone wrong. He looked at Julio, then Daniel, and finally Joe. "I don't like mistakes. If everyone stays with my plan, things will go perfectly."

Yolanda was confused. Was that last week? Where was she?

Her dream began again.

Sergio lifted his glass and said, "Here's to Yolanda. She managed to live one more week. If she learns to be obedient, she might get the rewards of the good life."

A loud noise from the kitchen interrupted his snide remarks. Everyone turned just in time to see their waiter collapse as he headed towards them.

In the confusion, (Yolanda had seen a few spy movies), she switched glasses with Joe, the nearest person. Joe stood up and said, "Here's to Sergio. May his plans always be perfect." He took one long sip and looked at Yolanda, puzzled about something. Then he pitched forward. Yolanda reached over and felt his pulse. There was nothing. She glanced at Sergio. He was furious. He stared at her as if she had killed Joe.

Daniel said, "Boss, I think we ought to go before the cops get called."

"Julio, go bring the car around. Daniel, help me carry Joe. Yolanda, act like he's had one too many and he's passed out."

No one seemed to notice as Joe was hustled out the door. Julio brought the car around and Joe was lowered to the back seat. Yolanda climbed in beside him to hold him upright.

Sergio said, "It wouldn't be good if I was caught with you. I'll meet you in about an hour at the compound." Sergio closed the door and walked away, talking on his cell phone.

Julio drove a few miles before turning down a dirt road. He pulled over at the first turnout. "That seems to happen when we're serious. Sergio avoids any chance of getting caught."

"Yolanda, we're going to put Joe in the trunk in case someone comes snooping."

Yolanda thought that was a dumb idea but she was afraid to disagree. She got out of the car and waited while Daniel and Julio stuffed Joe in the trunk. Yolanda started to close the trunk. Then everything went dark, at least until the spider began crawling across her face.

Now she was awake but helpless. Last week was the restaurant and this week the garden, or was it the other way around? Her head hurt. She must have hit her head. Sergio! Sergio was losing control more often. This time he meant to kill her. He would not try to make it up to her, give her gifts and apologize.

The voices were back. "The boss will be unhappy anyway so let's have fun with his wife before we see him. We'll say she almost got away and we had to dump her body in the river."

Yolanda began working on the tape on her wrists with renewed vigor. She was ready to give up but that spider on her neck was working its way back to her face. She had to get loose. If she calmed down she could think. The spider stopped. It had done its job for the moment. She was alert and able to communicate.

She had a strange peaceful feeling of being loved. Jose, Ramon, another being, and spirits of her ancestors. They were nearby. Animals were also near and ready to help. She had given up but now she was fighting for her life.

Jose was in his garden when a killdeer landed in front of him and began a broken wing dance. The bird got closer and closer. "That's really odd," he said out loud. "That's a dance usually reserved for times the babies are threatened." Then he suddenly became quiet and listened. The bird was telling him someone was in trouble.

"Show me the way!" he said.

Jose knew Ramon was in town and he stopped at Ramon's garden to see if Ramon was in trouble. Ramon was busily talking to Gabby. Jose motioned for both to get in the car.

As he drove Jose explained the situation. Jose followed the killdeer up a dirt road, driving carefully to avoid raising telltale clouds of dust. Both Jose and Ramon were silent. Both were angry and scared, afraid something had happened to Yolanda, Jose miserable because he wasn't protecting his mother and Ramon miserable because he was certain he had been a terrible father, neglecting his daughter while he concentrated on his career.

Just in case someone had been suspicious, Julio stopped at the side of the road. They waited, looking back to see if they had been followed. Both were cautious and ready for action if something went awry. "No one followed us," Daniel said. "We don't need to kill anyone right now. Maybe we can have some fun with this one.'

"We'll have to be careful. She's Sergio's woman. Just because he doesn't want her doesn't mean he will let anyone else have her."

Daniel glanced back and said, "I think I was wrong. We're gonna have company. I think a car is coming this way."

To prove his point Daniel pointed to the road behind them. A gray car was moving slowly towards them.

Daniel reached for his gun, intent on firing first and asking questions later. But just as he focused on the car, a red tail hawk barreled down from the sky. The hawk's talons raked across Daniel's bald head and across his nose. Blood spurted everywhere. "Get this thing off of me!" he screamed.

Another hawk joined in, its beak tearing chunks out of his ear. Daniel was in terror mode. He fired two shots in the air. Both hawks flew to the nearest tree. Daniel fired two more shots but the blood pouring from the wounds on his nose and ears distracted him.

A swarm of blue jays and mocking birds began their assault. They swooped and dove at Julio. Ducking and dodging, he was quickly overwhelmed. He tried to get into the car but the door wouldn't open. The birds continued to throw themselves against his face and his neck. "I can't breathe," he gasped as he ran for the woods swinging wildly. He almost made it to safety. As he gathered himself to leap into the woods he turned to see his tormentors. "Just little birds. They're not so scary." But when he turned back a large tree branch hit him square in the middle of his forehead and he dropped heavily to the ground.

Daniel was still firing imaginary bullets from an empty gun at an enemy he couldn't see. His blood had sealed his eyes shut. Ramon hit him with a branch and he fell to the ground.

Jose and Ramon ran to the car and opened the trunk. Yolanda was tied up with duct tape but unharmed. After releasing her, they collected the guns Daniel and Julio carried and searched the car for other weapons. The three of them pushed the car down a hill and against a chain link fence.

They left Julio and Daniel in the car, alive but unconscious. Ramon called the police and gave the location of the car. "There's been an accident. There's a car off the road and I think there are two people inside. I think both are injured." Ramon did not mention the body in the trunk.

Jose offered an apology for not protecting his mom. Ramon apologized profusely for not being a good father and for not being there for her.

"Papa, I never wanted to bother you. You always had important work to do. You had gardens to grow."

"Yolanda, you were more important than any garden. I could replace a garden but I could never replace you."

"I will listen to the spirits from now on. Both of you can also help protect me." They all knew without saying that sometime soon Sergio would search for Yolanda. He would not let her remain an example for others to emulate. She had to be taught to obey or he would never gain respect again.

Although Ramon vowed to be there for Yolanda, his life changed when he was promoted to executive vice president and moved to the Midwest, fifteen hundred miles away. He continued doing things he wanted to do except grow a garden. Life seemed dreary but he was convinced things would look brighter if he was successful with a garden, even a very small garden. He was determined to have fresh tomatoes and a few herbs. He babied his plants, gave them attention and nutrients, put them on his patio to discourage woodland herbivores. His vigilance seemed to work because nothing bothered his plants for months.

Change is always part of the equation. It's a variable that seems to occur when life gets too easy, or maybe it happens at the worst of times. Ramon was glad when his life began to smooth out. But that was when he noticed the changes that were happening in his body.

Ramon did not remember when his symptoms started. He guessed they began before he moved to Kansas City. He thought about his nights alone in his big house by the oak forest. Sometimes he would lie in bed waiting to sleep but his legs would not co-operate. The nerves were out of control, making his legs jump and twitch, reminding him of college science labs when he applied electrical currents to a frog's leg.

"Nervous Leg Syndrome," the science teacher had stated. "Someday some of you might have spasms just like these frogs. You will be jumping around without a clue. Go to a doctor."

Ramon didn't like to think of himself as a frog, especially one with nerves acting crazy. "I don't want to think about my science teacher. I'd rather think about angels".

But images of angels weren't making him sleepy either. In his dreams the angels carried electric prods and kept saying, "Be Good, Ramon. Be Good."

"O.k., angels. You've had your fun. Now let me sleep," Ramon grumbled.

His health was getting worse. He didn't feel well in the mornings and he rarely slept well. The muscles in his legs cramped often and he would have to massage his legs just so they could move. His feet were no longer dependable.

When he went for walks he would stumble over small rocks or twigs that were in his way. At first he laughed at his clumsiness. But when he stumbled more frequently he became concerned. He put off going to see his doctor because Ramon already had a solution. He decided his problems had to be stress related. If he relaxed more, surely the problems would go away.

To relax Ramon had several hobbies and interests that made him forget about work and the problems he encountered every day. He loved watching the wildlife from his dining room. He put up hummingbird feeders and scattered seeds for the cardinals, bluebirds, and blue jays. He tried to ignore the fox squirrels and gray squirrels as they jumped from branch to branch. He tried to drive the squirrels away from the seeds but the squirrels were persistent and would only leave and stay away if Ramon stood guard on his deck outside.

In the fall he also began to worry about the deer that came near his house. Where would they get enough feed to keep them during the winter? He bought a deer feeder and slid the box halfway down the hill before assembling it on a flat area. With a series of pulleys he pulled it upright and five feet off the ground. Then he secured it to the nearby trees. He made two more trips to get a bag of corn and a ladder.

Carefully he hoisted the bag of corn, cut the bag, and poured the corn into the feeder. He placed the lid on top and bolted it down. He placed a battery in the timer and set it.

After fifteen minutes the timer triggered a spinning device that scattered the corn in a circle beneath the feeder. Twenty minutes later the first deer were feeding on the corn. Every hour the timer released the spinner and more corn was dispersed. Deer walked over and began eating as soon as the spinner stopped. They waited patiently at first but as the number of deer increased, the waiting deer became more aggressive and were soon driving away their competition.

Some of his neighbors stopped by and pointed at the feeder. "What's that feeder doing so close to the houses? Hunters will be looking for easy targets and many won't care where the deer are. They'll shoot anything, even if the deer are on the decks."

Ramon hadn't thought of that. He was just trying to make sure the deer weren't hungry.

The oak and maple trees displayed their red and gold colors as fall rushed into the Midwest. The evening temperatures dropped into the upper twenties after Halloween and television weather forecasters were predicting possibilities of heavy snows. Ramon stocked up with supplies and prepared for closed stores and closed roads. His deck had several potted plants that he boasted were his miniature garden. Now he rushed to cover his four tomato plants, three pots with lettuce, two peppers and various herbs. There were enough kinds of familiar plants to spice up his tamales and enchiladas and remind him of mild winters ahead without the freezing winds or the sleet or snow. As he threw sheets and blankets over his small garden he remembered the forecast called for freezing temperatures when the sun set. His potted plants had gotten a late start and were just beginning to produce. One tomato was turning red and he planned to harvest it in the morning. He was excited that he still had his green thumb. Everything grew for him if he took good care of each plant.

Ramon took a few minutes to scan the ever changing landscape. His house, next to an oak forest, was in a beautiful location and he could see several deer scampering up a nearby hill. They appeared to be restless and he guessed they sensed the incoming storm. Ramon went inside and sat in his chair by the fire. In just a few minutes he was soon warm and asleep.

A slight noise woke him. Quietly he went upstairs and peered up the street. He rubbed his eyes. Was he still sleeping? Deer were everywhere. Two bucks were at the end of the cul-de-sac standing guard as other deer went from house to house, walking up the sidewalks and onto front porches, eating any plants within their reach.

Ramon watched for a few minutes before he slapped his forehead and said, "Holy cow!" and raced downstairs. The sheets and blankets were lying to one side of the patio. The pots were there but all leaves and fruits had been stripped from the plants. Only short stems were left.

Ramon raised his fists in the air. "You dumb deer! Those were my plants. I gave you corn. Grow your own garden!"

He realized the deer would not understand him and the neighbors would think he was crazy. He went inside and drank a cup of hot chocolate. Before he went to bed he looked outside. On the cement in front of one of his planters he saw the almost ripe tomato with two bites missing. He also made out the faint words, "I'm sorry," written with dirt. Ramon shook his head. "Those neighbor kids must have done this. I'll talk to them tomorrow."

A storm moved in that night and Ramon forgot his lost garden. He was determined to get to work. He refused to let the storm stop him even though his neighbors thought he was crazy. "Wait for the salt and sand," they cautioned. "The roads are treacherous and icy. You could be killed if you make one mistake."

He didn't enjoy winters like he once did. The roads worried him, not because he wasn't cautious but because other drivers took too many chances. He vowed this would be his final winter in heavy coats, shoveling snow and watching the weather channel for updates and emergencies. His knees were continually aching, his feet swollen, and his lungs burned when he stayed too long outside.

His physical problems were not his only complaints. He felt lonely and alone. His friends had deserted him. Wintertime reminded him that he was getting old and his days of visiting friends would soon be over. He wondered if it was time to retire and move to a retirement community.

He didn't wait long. A few nights later he dreamed about a huge garden and plants of every kind. He was perspiring as the sun beamed down. He was singing and happy. "This is the life," he told himself. "Life must be tasted and enjoyed. All work and no friends will kill me."

When the winter storms were at their worst, Ramon strolled into the main office and submitted his resignation. "It's time for the young folks to take over. I need to rest."

Green Thumb

I've always wanted a green thumb,
So I could grow plants from seeds.
Though I tried methods old and new,
The ones that grew best were weeds.
All my life I tried to improve the soil,
But there was little I could do about it.
I watered the plants with sweat and tears
They wouldn't have grown without it.
It took me years to find my touch,
Until my garden went on a growing spree.
Proudly I stood and admired the sprouts,
Vowing nothing would ever stop me.
I'll never prove I've got a green thumb.
The ground is bare as far as I can see.
Critters and bugs devoured it all,
And they might be the death of me.

Before he could get away from the company, disaster struck. Two of the top executives were injured in a terrible automobile accident. Ramon was asked to fill in and take over their responsibilities while they recovered. Because he was the only one who understood the company's growth and what they were trying to accomplish, Ramon felt compelled to say yes.

For the next eight months Ramon drove himself relentlessly, putting in fourteen to sixteen hours daily. Under his leadership the company grew and prospered. New customers were anxious to try new crops and new foods and he had the inside track. He spent long hours at the lab experimenting with combinations of plants from Aztec gardens and modern biogenetics. He made new discoveries and soon countries and individuals were making new demands on his time.

He rushed from job to job trying to please everyone and make his discoveries count. He still suffered from stress and depression. Perhaps he was too tired because he thought more and more about death. He still wrote in his journal, writing to himself, writing how he felt.

DEAD TIME

Nothing is happening
Except on the morning news
All is quiet around me
While the rest of the world stews.
Death is striking quickly
Coming from out of the blue,
I feel your agony, world
Because I'm dying too.
I'd like to taste death
After one final fling,
Death would be sweeter
And lose its last sting.

He looked tired and acted tired when he was at work. The CEO knocked on his door early one morning and said, "Ramon. You're working too hard. Take a vacation. Everything will still be here when you come back."

After a long discussion, Ramon agreed to take one week off but living by the forest had spoiled him. Where could he go and be happier?

He tried golf and fishing. "I can't concentrate," he insisted. "How can I do nothing while people are starving?" he asked.

His friends invited him to meet at bars but that was not his style. If he was going to party he would call his relatives and have a fiesta. But now he wanted to relax and think about his daughter and Jose.

Out of exasperation they asked him to join a reading group at the library. On a table a copy of Organic Gardening caught his eye. "That's what I need. I used to enjoy working with the soil and finding ways to make it come alive. I've got two more days before I return to work. I'll visit a farm."

He visited a friend who grew cotton on a large ranch. His friend was very informative but he could not convince Ramon that cotton was the crop of the future. "The poor can't eat cotton," Ramon told his friend.

There was an excuse for each kind of farm. Orange trees took too long to grow. Rice grew in water. Wheat needed too many steps to process. Walnut trees had to be shaken and were unbearably dusty. Grapes were delicate and temperamental. None were what he wanted. Maybe he could interest others in chia seeds, the power seeds of Aztec warriors.

"I want something more basic. Different vegetables, making rows, watering, and gathering the fruits off their vines. No complications, no stress, just me lazily watching the plants grow."

Ramon didn't like having a vacation because it only reminded him of the things he wanted to do and it reminded him that his health was failing and his life was getting shorter.

Four years had passed quickly and he had not been successful with his attempts at gardening. Too much sun, too much rain, too much snow. It had all been just too much. Gardening required attention and he had been too busy at work to keep his plants on schedules that suited their needs.

He had much to share with Yolanda and Jose. It was time to quit and get control of his life again. He submitted his resignation but agreed to be a consultant from time to time.

On his last day of work Ramon's co-workers marched into the staff room singing, "For he's a jolly good fellow, for he's a jolly good fellow, for he's a jolly good fellow, that no one can deny."

There were those who envied him and were adamant that he would miss them and the company right from the start. Others whispered behind his back and said he was too old and cranky. It really didn't matter what anyone said. He was now officially retired and glad that it was all over. No longer was he confined to small office spaces with the phone constantly ringing. The gloomy forecasts of a failing economy and running his days by a clock were done. That lifestyle was over and he could return to his roots.

For months he had dreamed of working in the great outdoors. He yearned for a job that allowed freedom of movement and fresh air. His Aztec ancestors knew more than he thought they did. Their lifestyle kept them healthy and content.

During this time of discontent Ramon's relatives urged him to move from the cold and return to the land of gold. "California is the place to be, Ramon," they insisted. "The weather won't control what you want to do."

Two weeks later he was on a train going west to the wide open spaces. The Amtrak locomotive rolled day and night, stopping only to load or unload passengers. Once, though, the train stopped late in the night.

The power went off for forty minutes and Ramon was curious. "What's the reason the power went off?" he inquired.

"The train hit an animal on the tracks and the train needed to be cleaned," one of the conductors told him discretely. "Tomorrow we will have a special change in the menu."

The lights came on again and the train continued through New Mexico and Arizona. At lunch there was an addition to the menu and the conductor leaned down and whispered, "Road kill. Probably an antelope being chased by Aztec hunters drove the animal into the train."

The conductor's statement startled Ramon. "Why did you say that?" Ramon asked.

"I believe I have some Aztec blood. My mother used to say our ancestors will show up in times of trouble. We need to be reminded of our strengths and our weaknesses from time to time. On this trip I've been feeling another presence. Someone on this train is full of the ancient power. I hope that man or woman isn't here because of something bad, like an accident, that's going to happen."

Ramon tried to sleep after lunch and he paid little attention to the landscape. It was not green and lush like he wanted. It appeared to be dry and hostile. He didn't notice the train's speed gradually increasing as they got closer to civilization.

The conductor rushed by. "We're going too fast for the curve coming up. Keep your luggage compartment closed and your head down!"

Ramon closed his eyes and imagined thousands of warriors straining against the train, slowing it down. The train groaned and strained to stay on the tracks. Slowly it lost speed and came to a stop. The conductor walked by again. "I don't understand it. The brakes weren't working properly and then suddenly they were. We're safe. I need a vacation and time to relax."

When Ramon disembarked in Los Angeles he walked past a sign that read, "Where water flows, everything grows!" The sign inspired him. He would grow everything! There were no limits! He would grow gardens like the ones his mother grew when he was a child. His garden would be even bigger and better. All he had to do was to watch out for neighborhood children. They might destroy his plants just like the children in the forest had done.

Everything started out great. Ramon's older brother offered Ramon a large area to begin his garden. "It's got water. It's got a six foot chain link fence all around it. I've got two German Shepherd dogs that will chase everything away. This area is better protected than Fort Knox.

The soil is clay and hard to work with but I'll bet you have already planned out your strategy. If you do things right and give the plants proper amounts of water they will grow. By the way, which strategy are you using? Mom's way, the way of our ancestors or the modern way of chemicals and poisons?"

His brother didn't say their dad's way or Ramon's way. No, he didn't. But he did hint very strongly which way he preferred.

Ramon wanted to say 'the modern way' but he knew he would be disagreeing just for the sake of argument. He agreed most of the time with his ancestors and maybe even more. The Aztecs had experimented with plants long before other tribes thought of improving their crops and gardens.

His brother's words made it seem so easy to get the garden started. Ramon noticed that his brother was not offering to help in any way. Ramon didn't want to argue the merits of any kind of gardening so he said quietly, "This is going to be a piece of cake."

It wasn't long before Ramon discovered how wrong he had been. He thrust the shovel at the ground expecting the blade to slice deep and cut out a large chunk of earth. Instead, the shovel bounced back, jarring him to his core. The shovel made little impact on the hard clay. He jumped on the shovel's blade but again the soil resisted his efforts.

Ramon groaned and redoubled his efforts but the shovel only went in two inches before hitting hard pan. His misery was lost in the dry air because he was the only living creature around, except the ground squirrels and rabbits.

Perhaps the spirits of his ancestors were listening. "How will my garden grow in this inhospitable place?" he asked out loud. No one answered so Ramon decided that the spirits were sleeping or didn't care. After all, he had chosen the modern way and had rejected the past.

Nearby in a field across a rural highway, cows were straining to reach taller grass on the other side of the fence. Ramon watched them for a few minutes before he burst out laughing. Two of the cows were standing side by side chewing contentedly, their heads caught between two wooden rails. They were not trying to get free. They were patiently waiting for someone to release them from their self-imposed jail. Ramon noted, "Somehow cows seem to get themselves in predicaments. They're always thinking of their four stomachs instead of being smart."

Green patches of grass dotted the dry field where the herd of cows was standing. Ramon was suddenly inspired. "Fertilizer! That's the answer. Fertilizer and leaves and grass. That will help loosen the soil and retain moisture. The roots of plants will have a chance to spread out. Maybe my garden will grow if I mix everything in and keep the soil cultivated."

Ramon began searching the classified ads in his local newspaper. There were no ads listing cow manure for sale so he spent the next three days visiting nearby farms. At first he had no success but the word got out quickly. The third evening of his search Ramon received a phone call from a rancher who lived five miles from town. "Would you be willing to work for horse manure?" a voice asked.

Ramon borrowed a truck. Soon Ramon was shoveling out stalls and cleaning out the rancher's barn. The manure was loaded onto the truck, brought to his garden area, and spread out across the garden plot. Ramon's shoulders and back ached after each work session. He tried to divide his time between the horse ranch and his garden. After three days the truck was emptied, cleaned, and returned. The two men shook hands, glad to do business with each other. Each man left with a smile, one with a clean barn and stalls, the other with several inches of mature covering his prospective garden.

Ramon hired two young men to move and spread the manure. Wheelbarrow after wheelbarrow brought the fertilizer to strategic spots. Afterwards, the rototiller mixed the fertilizer and soil as it began churning the soil. Ramon and his helpers made rows from west to east so each row would get the benefits from the sun.

As they spread seeds in each row Ramon noticed the birds gathering on the telephone and electric lines. The birds watched without making noise at first but then curiosity got the better of them. They moved to the chain link fence that surrounded the garden and finally they were on the ground hopping around looking for seeds and worms. They eyed Ramon suspiciously at first, expecting him to come charging at them. When they were ignored, their circle tightened. Behind them the squirrels were coming closer and closer, afraid to miss out on any treat or any kind of action.

The two young men had brought two dogs to keep all animals away from the plot. The dogs would run at the birds and squirrels occasionally, but that game became too hot under the sun.

The next morning the men arrived at seven, two hours earlier when it was a lot cooler. The dogs were anxious to begin and soon they chased one rabbit away and into the empty field next to the garden. Ramon tried to ignore what the dogs were doing because he was busy trying to drive the birds and squirrels away.

The rabbit appeared again, right beside the dogs. Ramon wondered if the rabbit stuck out its tongue or talked trash about how slow they were because the dogs were immediately in hot pursuit.

Ramon watched the dogs chasing the rabbit for over fifteen minutes. The rabbit and the dogs had peculiar patterns in the ways they ran. The dogs would split up and the faster dog would drive the rabbit towards the second dog which waited in the pathway of the rabbit. When the rabbit ran approximately two hundred feet, the rabbit would reverse directions. The chasing dog would skid to a stop and race after the rabbit. The second dog waited until the last moment and leaped into the air, snapping furiously. Always the dog was just a little bit late with its timing. It never got a taste of rabbit.

This game continued for thirty minutes without stopping. The dogs were sweaty and tiring fast. The rabbit appeared to be fresh and having fun. "There's something wrong with this picture," Ramon thought. He slipped behind a tree nearby that had a better angle.

Ramon could see the rabbit increase its lead before it dove into the brush. The dogs would sniff the brush, the rabbit would race back with the dogs in hot pursuit. Three times Ramon watched the procedure. The rabbit looked different the third time. Ramon scratched his head. What was going on? Then Ramon understood. When the rabbit dove into the brush, an exchange was made. Another rabbit would jump out and race to the other pile of brush. Another rabbit would jump out and the cycle continued until the dogs were exhausted and crashed to the ground. The rabbits were running in relays and were running for fun.

Ramon knew the dogs had been outsmarted. Now the dogs were utterly exhausted and would have to be carried back to the parking lot.

The two young men came for their dogs. "What happened to them?" one asked. "We've never seen them this tired."

Ramon shrugged his shoulders and said, "The dogs must have had too much fun chasing rabbits. With a little rest your dogs will be good as new."

The two young men urged the dogs to get up. Finally they bent down and each man picked up a dog. As they stumbled to their car, they did not see the rabbits dancing behind them. Neither did they see the rabbits giving each other high fives and waving their ears in salute.

The rabbits turned and winked at Ramon. Then they disappeared into the brush and within a minute there was nothing moving, nothing racing, and nothing hopping anywhere.

Ramon should have known better than to begin his garden without getting rid of the birds, the squirrels, and the rabbits. He prepared the ground and added fertilizer and mulch. He placed chicken wire around the base of his fence to keep out intruders. Netting was over the strawberries. Ramon had tested the soil, gotten the best seeds, and set up a drip irrigation system.

Everything was perfect. It was the Garden of Eden revisited. Ramon did not plan for the craftiness and tenacity of all the vermin. The animals had joined in a conspiracy that would drive him crazy. And if animals didn't drive him loco, people would.

NO RAIN IN SIGHT

The crickets were forecasting the weather last night,
Singing, "No rain in sight! No rain in sight!"
Wells are drying up, businesses are shutting down,
Soon no one will be living in this deserted town.
And today two men were chastised for washing their car.
I've got to escape real soon to someplace real far.

My friends are looking at me with evil in their eyes.
My well is still working but I'm beginning to tell lies.
If they only knew I took a bath last night,
They'd sputter and yell and say it wasn't right.
Then one and all would leave with a frown,
And sometime in the night my house might burn down.
I've got to be careful when crickets sing their song.
Anything I say might be construed as wrong.
Especially when the dust hangs heavy in the air.
There's no rain in sight, so beware, beware!

Ramon knew water was scarce and he carefully wrote down in his journal each time he watered and the times he started and finished. His plants were still green and growing, the mulch and fertilizer holding the moisture for longer periods of time. Because his garden was lush and green, neighbors and friends were very envious of his success and insisted he must be using more than his share of water.

Ramon remembered the sign in the train depot. "Where water flows, everything grows." 'This drought should be over soon', he reasoned. "I'll just have be careful with my irrigation." He did not check with the weather channel or weather experts that studied long term weather patterns.

Ramon labored in the sun, lovingly and carefully placing the seeds and plants in meticulous rows or circular patterns. He did not pay close attention to the eyes that watched hungrily. He was in charge and he would maintain order as the tomatoes, the cantaloupes, the beans and watermelons, and the other assorted vegetables grew in precise formations. In theory, Ramon's garden should be the best one around.

At first the plants themselves did not co-operate. They were unruly. They grew rapidly, sprawling over cages and netting. Ramon adjusted his watering and feeding schedules. There were timelines and soil and fertilizer mixtures adjusted for each type of plant. Ramon worked the garden methodically, expecting everything to grow exactly as he wanted. He made several mistakes even though he wanted everything to be perfect. The biggest mistake was in thinking he was in charge and he could control everything. He did not consult Yolanda or his ancestor spirits and therefore he was on his own. He also did not consider the many ways the critters could invade his garden.

THE INVASION BEGINS

One morning Ramon noticed the cantaloupe vines were lying in new directions. He scratched his head and studied them. As he pondered, one vine stretched taut and then suddenly went limp. Ramon walked over and examined the end of the vine. It had been sliced cleanly. Something had happened in plain sight and he had missed it.

Ramon focused on a small hill and was rewarded when a pair of ears emerged, followed by a pair of dark eyes. A rabbit stared at him unflinching, apparently waiting for his next move. Ramon was certain the rabbit was smiling as it began munching cantaloupe vines. The rabbit appeared to be unconcerned with Ramon's presence. Either the rabbit was very brave or it realized Ramon had no chance of catching it.

Like a soldier preparing to march off to battle, Ramon swung his hoe up and against his shoulder all the while muttering angrily, "Mister Rabbit, this means war!"

Ramon strode purposely toward the rabbit but the rabbit remained still until Ramon was closing in. Then with three short hops the rabbit disappeared under the fence. Ramon was fuming because the rabbit had violated the security of the garden and had tarnished his image of Eden, his model of perfection.

Once safe with the fence between them, the rabbit turned and winked. It was deliberate and mean spirited. Ramon knew this rabbit was taunting him but there was nothing he could do. The rabbit waved, but not at Ramon. Expecting the worst, Ramon turned around slowly. Behind him little rabbits were munching on cantaloupe flowers and new growth of other plants.

Ramon lifted his hoe and the rabbits scattered in all directions. He was like the legendary Mr. McGregor chasing Peter Rabbit. Ramon was too slow and the rabbit wriggled under the gate and escaped.

THE ATTACK OF THE HUNGRY HORDES

Over the next four days Ramon fixed the fence, set traps, and even put out rabbit repellant. He was determined to keep the rabbits away. The ground squirrels used the fence as a jungle gym or part of an obstacle course. They could climb anything or dig tunnels that went under. The traps were baited to lure squirrels or rabbits inside cages. If any had been captured Ramon would have taken the prisoners a few miles away and released them but none took the bait. The rabbit repellent was harmless to critters. Its main ingredient was coyote urine. Ramon was the only one that hated the smell.

Throughout the summer Ramon waged war but it became clear he was on the losing side. With the exception of the tomatoes, his garden was getting smaller under the attack of the hungry hordes.

Each night Ramon had nightmares about rabbits and ground squirrels. In his dreams rabbits and squirrels sat at a huge banquet table eating their fill while he hurried to grow more to satisfy their needs. Each rabbit and squirrel told others and soon cousins and uncles and other kin arrived from distant climes to share this ongoing feast.

Rabbits were everywhere and thrived despite his best efforts. Ramon finally capitulated and left the rabbits and squirrels alone. Ramon's dreams convinced him they were the chosen ones.

It seemed no matter what Ramon did, the vegetables disappeared at an alarming rate. The relatives that had been invited by other ground squirrels or rabbits were coming to the garden after hours and taking more than their share.

The garden war intensified. The rabbits responded to Ramon's efforts to drive them away. No longer did they simply hide behind the plants and run if discovered. Now the squirrels and rabbits were becoming mischievous. Despite Ramon's best efforts at controlling the border of his garden with fencing, it went for naught.

The attacks on the garden increased on all fronts. The cute little bunnies enlisted the help of gophers to assist the ground squirrels. Instead of holes here and there that the rabbits and squirrels could dive into, the gophers constructed a massive labyrinth. With that tunnel system being convenient at every location, the critters could appear and disappear at will. Under all the stress Ramon began creating little rhymes.

THEY KEEP ON MUNCHING

Ramon went around muttering one of his favorite rhymes. "Hop, hop, hop. They keep on munching and never stop."

An aerial attack was also underway. Doves, pigeons, and blue jays swooped down on the strawberries, selecting the ripest and plumpest for casual eating, and disdainfully rejecting the berries with flaws. The birds shredded the lettuce and made the rest of the garden almost inedible.

Ramon tied colorful streamers to poles, hoping that the motions of the aluminum strips fluttering in the breeze would startle the birds and keep them away. However, the multi-colored strips attracted large flocks of birds, ravenous after flying around searching for food.

Ramon was certain most of those birds had arrived from the airport nearby. Perhaps the streamers reminded the birds of wind socks, letting the incoming traffic land without mishap. In any case Ramon thought the combined forces presented an overwhelming battle front.

For awhile Ramon hated all the opposing critters because they had taken charge and eliminated any chance of a successful harvest.

Ramon yelled at them frequently. "You're greedy and selfish. You're destroying everything. Have you no decency?"

Privately he wished all of the critters would overeat and pop. But nothing happened. Ramon could see the chubby rabbits hopping between rows with no regard for his needs. Ramon always watched and waited. He still couldn't catch them on open ground, but if one critter got careless, He might catch a rabbit or squirrel and have stew.

Ramon waited for his chance but his heart softened as he began to observe their habits and traits. All rabbit and squirrel families were not the same. For example, he saw some families stop at the gate or at the fence. The mothers would gather their families and explain why they needed to behave while they were shopping. There were other critter families that released their charges as soon as they got close. The wee rabbits and squirrels scampered around wildly without regard for others. Not only were the little rabbits a distraction to other shoppers, but they were often in harm's way. But whether the animal mothers allowed wild hares or not, Ramon realized how similar to humans the animal families were. He could not think about harming them after that.

Ramon thought about gardens during the day and dreamed about gardens at night. His dreams became more confusing as reality and fantasy blended. His father would have ridiculed him if he had known about the animals who were becoming more real with each passing dream.

In his journal Ramon wrote about the rabbits who had taken over his garden. They had names and carried on conversations. They were more than cartoon characters. They weren't his friends but now he was beginning to understand them.

He imagined their activities in very human terms. He wrote the following poem in his journal.

The Garden of Diminishing Returns

There were cantaloupes, squash, tomatoes galore,
Green beans, watermelons, green peppers and more,
Growing fast, trying to crawl out of sight,
I thought I could hear the garden growing at night,
But in the mornings when I checked the plants,
The vegetables were half eaten and covered with ants,
No matter what I tried or wherever I turned,

The results were the same----diminishing returns!
I sat out in my chair with my dog on the lawn,
Hoping to see some critters, I'd wait until dawn,
Ground squirrels were scurrying, rabbits came dancing,
Cicadas were chirping, deer were prancing,
Everywhere I looked there was some kind of motion,
The garden was alive with activity and commotion,
Chomping new flowers and munching new shoots,
The animals were all dressed in their evening suits,
There was a call to order and they all sat down,
The biggest rabbit was worried, I could tell by his frown,
"We've got to control the rabbits at school,
There's been multiplication against the rule,
Not everyone stays seated until a lesson is through,
This is outrageous! What shall we do?
Deer have been entering and then going out,
I'm not sure what's that all about,
And the squirrels have been going nuts,
So there you have it, no ifs, ands, or buts,
We'll have to move on and find new grounds,
This garden will be tagged as "out of bounds",
But if we destroy too much we'll soon learn,
One small garden yields diminishing returns,"
They thumped out a vote and gave him a hand,
It was clear they agreed with his conservative stand,
The majority was liberal enough to see,
If they harvested carefully enough there'd be,
If each did his share, working part of each day,
There would also be time to sleep and play,
He explained if they wanted, they could help him with stuff,
So they planted, watered, and did more than enough.
He told them that they still had lots to learn,

Because no one wins with diminishing returns.
That old rabbit spoke with authority before he
disappeared underground,
I'm glad I stayed alert and wrote it all down.
That garden was a life source to all, including me,
It brought a new way of thinking for us to get along,
And I really like those critters, don't get me wrong.
But if someone thinks I'm feeding that complete herd,
That's way out of line, kind of crazy, absurd!
Okay, just a nibble. I grew tons of stuff.
If all of you are careful there's more than enough!

The sprinklers went off and woke me from a dream,
I can't quite remember what made me want to scream.
But now I have a peaceful feeling way deep inside,
And when I look at my garden I have a sense of pride.
Every row is trimmed, organized, and neat,
But I could almost swear I see some little feet.
My garden is growing right up to the sky,
And on my doorstep this morning was a
strawberry pie.
I always thought gardening would be hard to learn,
Because I heard there was a problem with diminishing
returns.

Each day Ramon would scan his journal to see if there was a trend or pattern to his madness. Was he losing his mind or had he lost his mind long ago? Logically he could not justify what had been happening. What if he explained his world to his friends or his doctors? What if someone told him things from life that were equally fantastic? Would he believe what he was told?

THE NEGOTIATED SETTLEMENT

Ramon leaned on his hoe and thought about all that had transpired that summer and the summer before. He was tired of being soft with the rabbits. They weren't cute little bunny rabbits. His opinion had changed again because a new leader of the rabbits had taken control.

Ramon and the new leader had very little in common and very little they could agree upon regarding the garden. Ramon had lost the war in the trenches and his vegetables were disappearing at an alarming rate under the onslaught of the rabbits. In reality he had already conceded and the rabbits knew they were too much for him.

Ramon toyed with the idea of putting poison in every hole he found, hoping the rabbits would eat and die. But the poison would have caused long slow deaths for the rabbits and possibly for dogs or cats that happened upon a weakened rodent and decided it was a snack. Ramon could not take a chance.

Another alternative was for Ramon to sit outside with his shotgun and shoot at least one. He could not do either because both plans had flaws. He could be fined or arrested for shooting a firearm too close to residences. He didn't want to disturb his neighbors with the noise. Already they complained about shots being fired in the neighborhood. And he did not want to accidently shoot himself during all of the excitement.

Ramon sat down and leaned against a tree, pondering the ultimate demise of the pesky critters. His eyelids were heavy and he closed his eyes just for the moment. He was so tired and needed to rest. It seemed like he was floating but the tree was keeping him anchored to one spot. He hadn't moved but now he could see and hear things he had missed before.

Off in the distance a strange cadence broke the silence. The noise grew louder and Ramon decided it was coming his way. He recognized the sound just as a line of rabbits came thumping and hopping into view. It was a parade that almost defied description.

Every rabbit carried a musical instrument. Ramon counted twenty trombones, twenty trumpets, fifteen snare drums, ten clarinets, ten saxophones, and twenty flutes. At first only the drummers were playing as they turned and marched past Ramon. Then the band came to a halt right in front of Ramon. A tall rabbit raised his hand, and waited just until he had attention of the musicians. Then with graceful motions he directed a beautiful Souza march.

Behind the musical marchers were three rows of suited rabbits. Ramon was impressed by their similar appearances. Their ears stood tall and proud, their button noses were still, and their demeanor relaxed. They wore crisp pin-striped suits and looked like they were fresh out of Entrepreneur or Gentleman's Quarterly. They began marching in place before separating and forming a pathway to let one of the suited rabbits through.

A grizzled old rabbit stepped forward and leaned on his polished cane. "Son," he muttered, "we're here to negotiate a truce. With all the fighting lately none of us can enjoy the fruits of our labor. The vegetables will be gone soon if nothing is done. I'm here to help you."

Ramon's face registered the shock of the lawyer's words. Ramon scratched his head. Why did the rabbits want to help him? He was considered the enemy.

Two rabbits pulled papers from their briefcases and handed them to the old lawyer. He glanced at the papers before clearing his throat. "Everybody listen. We think everyone could benefit from our proposal."

Ramon thought it over quickly. This was his chance to get out of all these garden wars. Ramon took a deep breath and began. "It's my garden so I'm willing to give the rabbits and squirrels ten percent. No, make that twenty percent." He was feeling generous and happy his ordeal was over.

The old lawyer chuckled a little and then he thumped the ground, howling with laughter. Other rabbits joined in and laughed even harder until the old rabbit raised a paw and bade them to stop.

"There are so many more of us and we need more because of our sheer numbers. We think the split should be different than what you have pictured. You have put us under mental stress because you raised our standard of living and now you're trying to get out of our implied contract. Shame on you! Our little ones will have to take the brunt of your refusal to keep us healthy and happy. Therefore if it please the court we will see justice done. Our proposal is for us to receive ninety percent and for this gentleman to receive ten percent. That's twice as much as he needs. In addition we also expect him to maintain the garden in order to earn his ten percent. To be fair, for our part we will eat the grass and thin the vegetables."

"That's not fair," Ramon fumed. "That's robbery!"

The old rabbit frowned at his assistants. All were solemn as they looked at Ramon. Except for an occasional nose twitch none moved. The rabbit looked again at Ramon. "You have no choice. Take us to court or accept our terms now. Take it or leave it. We might decide to take it all!"

He stomped out of the garden, stopping only for a moment to give the papers back to his aides. He whispered to his assistants. They hopped about nervously, occasionally frowning at Ramon, before the rabbits slipped out the gate and into the night.

While Ramon considered the old lawyer's offer, a young rabbit pushed against the garden fence, looking for a place to enter. "This is ridiculous," Ramon stated. "They've gotten so fat they can't get in."

The negotiation process seemed very corrupt and it seemed that Ramon had nothing to bargain with. He would lose everything or get ten percent, if he worked hard. If he didn't act quickly he could lose even the ten percent.

He decided to agree with the terms as presented. The settlement was not right but Ramon did not want to argue anymore. This year he was beaten.

Ramon shook himself. He must have been dreaming and having a nightmare. An idea was now taking shape. Ramon smiled.

"Next year," he told himself. "Next year I will win. I will thwart all attacks because I won't care. I will plant weeds."

Ramon smiled at his devilish plan. He'd win by losing. He wouldn't have a garden but the critters and the lawyers would get nothing! It was brilliant!

THE CELEBRATION

It was a black tie event, a celebration for winning the garden wars. Invitations went out far and wide, and those in the know were hoping to be included in this once in a lifetime celebration. Never before had the rabbits taken a garden by storm, negotiated an agreement with major implications for all rabbits everywhere.

On the invitation a brief paragraph explained the special circumstances of the garden wars. No shots had been fired and consequently there were no deaths. Dinner, dancing, two guest speakers, and two singers were on the agenda. There was plenty of time to round up bunny sitters, dates if needed, and time to work the press into a frenzy. For rabbits, it was the place to be.

The bucks were dressed from head to toe,
Hat, tie, tux, proud enough to crow.
Their ladies were fluffed and beautiful,
Swaying, strutting, and putting on a show.
Gabby was waiting tables,
Trying not to stare.
The guests pretended to ignore him,
As if they didn't care.

After a salad from Ramon's garden, the waiters brought out eggplant parmesan, borsch, and pizza. There was no need to question whether the dishes were meatless. The guests would have choked at the mere suggestion that meat was part of the meal.

When dinner was over and the tables cleared, stacked, and carried out, the emcee, Grandpa Rabbit, introduced two speakers, Ernest and Gabby, two outstanding young rabbits. He noted that each one would make a short presentation before the dancing began.

Ernest stepped to the microphone and said,
"Gabby is a singer of songs, a teller of tales,
The vision he sees, he claims must prevail.
For our proud clan to give in to fears,
Would set us back many hard fought years.
I think we should throw him out,
Before his rantings fill us with doubt."

The crowd applauded and asked for more, but the emcee insisted no encore.

Gabby stood up and straightened his coat, shook his head and cleared his throat.

We might say we won and continue to fight,
But did we relax and sleep well at night?
Nobody wins until a war finally ends,
Then we can return to being good friends.
I have a friend I want you to meet,
He'll keep you dancing and on your feet.

Jose emerged from a nearby tree and before anyone could object or flee,

He began with the bunny hop. There was no way they could stop.

The event was a success even though a human, considered by many to be an enemy, supplied the evening entertainment.

ANOTHER PROBLEM: CHICKENS!

Diminishing returns, negotiated settlements, and wars with the squirrels and rabbits worried Ramon throughout the fall and winter. He finally came up with a new strategy. Rather than continuing the fight he would work with Jose and Yolanda and form a family cooperative.

Ramon didn't know it but the rabbits weren't his only problem. A new foe loomed before him. His friend, John, the owner of the land Ramon was working, had been away on a trip. In John's absence, his son, Tom, had become used to being in charge. One early summer morning a pickup came roaring up the driveway and stopped beside the garden.

Ramon was around the corner of the shed, hoeing weeds and creating straight furrows for the water to flow efficiently. Because he was keeping a wary eye out for the ravenous rabbits, his attention was diverted and he didn't comprehend the drastic changes taking place a few feet away. Tom's pickup was loaded with crates of chickens. There were white Leghorns, Rhode Island reds, barred Plymouth Rock chickens, and Araunas. As Tom unloaded the crates he was rough and bounced the crates around. The chickens protested loudly.

Ramon's view was blocked by the shed and the pickup but the sounds of the chickens shrieking and complaining caught his ear.

"But, but, but—this spot? But, but, but---this spot?" the chickens sputtered.

Ramon understood them and that confused him even more. He wasn't used to the ancient powers. He wasn't supposed to hear and understand animals. He was from the modern world, where facts, not feelings, controlled the world. He did not follow the path his mother wanted him to take.

"But, but, but---this spot?" The clamor continued to build. "I think I know what to do!" the roosters crowed.

Ramon peered around the corner. Chickens were all over the garden. Some were chasing bugs. Others were shredding the tops of leafy plants. One group scratched at the ground, doing a dance of some kind. And yet another group practiced flying over the garden, diving low, then gaining altitude and stopping to land on anything higher than the ground.

Shocked to see this army of intruders, Ramon staggered back a few steps. "Where did these chickens come from? Why are they here?"

At that time Tom shouted, "Isn't this great? The chickens will eat all of the bugs in your garden and I won't even have to buy chicken feed."

Ramon watched in horror as the chickens hunted for bugs, pecked at strawberries, poked holes in the tomatoes, tore gaping holes in the lettuce and cabbage leaves, and left their droppings everywhere.

"Isn't this great?" Tom repeated. "Now you won't have to worry about bugs."

"They're destroying everything," Ramon protested. His garden was in chaos and under attack once more.

Tom glared at Ramon. "But I thought you'd be happy with my surprise. You don't even seem grateful that I'm helping you with your garden."

"Get your chickens out of here! Your dad said no one would interfere with my garden. Where is he? We need to discuss this!" Ramon's blood pressure was rising. This garden was intended to reduce his tensions and help him relax but things were definitely going wrong.

Tom was irritated. "You are not appreciating my efforts. Think about the money I'll make on eggs. I've already promised my friends that they would be getting eggs cheaper from me than at the store.

You're being very selfish, Ramon. I told Dad that he couldn't trust you. You're getting to use this plot for free and you're not even grateful. I bought these chickens for you. Now it's your responsibility to take care of them."

As Tom climbed into his pickup he said several disrespectful phrases about Ramon, then revved his engine and sped off, throwing gravel and dirt all over.

Ramon sat on the ground, his hands on his head, worrying. What was he going to do with forty chickens? He didn't know the exact number because they never stopped long enough for him to count. They were too busy chasing bugs, snipping off tender buds and shoots, and scratching out holes in the ground. Ramon was too old to cry so he tried to relax and meditate, hoping he could ignore his problems for awhile.

A soft voice caught his attention. "Tiene una problema, Papa?"

Ramon turned and saw Yolanda smiling down at him. "Can I help you?" she asked.

Ramon had always taken care of his own problems. He always refused outside help because he liked being independent. But this time was different. He was exhausted. There was too much commotion and everything was spinning out of control.

"Yolanda, what can I do about these chickens?" he asked. "I want order, not chaos!"

The chickens were out of control, running from one spot to another. There was no simple solution to catching them.

"Papa, you've always made me stay in the present, not using the ancient spirits. We can wait until dark when the chickens naturally roost, I can have the spirits drive the chickens to one corner of the garden and we can catch them, or you can talk to the chickens yourself."

"I don't talk to the spirit world or have conversations with animals, Yolanda. You know that."

"Papa, I know you haven't, but I know you can. You've been listening to animals lately. I can see your reactions. Grandmother said your skills were dormant but not erased. She said you could use them if a need came up. She said you were gifted."

"Yolanda, will you ask the chickens to eat the bugs around the house and the garden but leave the plants alone?"

"I could, Papa, but I won't. It will be better if you develop your own relationship with the chickens. It'll mean so much more to all of you."

Ramon frowned and walked to the center of the garden and began to chant. The chickens stared at him at first, frozen for the moment. Then one by one their eyes glazed over and began to cluck along with Ramon. "Cluck, cluck. Cluck, cluck." They began moving out of the garden and spreading into the field. Soon Ramon could hear them clucking, "We can do it. We can do it. We will find the bugs and keep your garden safe."

Ramon thought his troubles were over regarding the chickens but that afternoon John arrived in his work car. It had numerous dents and places where gray primer had been brushed on and was easily recognized. Ramon gave a friendly wave when John stopped beside the garden.

John slowly emerged from his car. Ramon noticed he had been drinking and he wasn't smiling. "Say, Ramon, I heard you and Tom had a discussion about the garden." His voice was hard and mean. "Tom says he was doing you a favor and you lost your cool. You insisted he keep his chickens out of your garden. Ramon, I said you could use this ground for free, but I can't have you bullying my son. I hope this kind of incident never happens again. You know what I mean, mi compadre? Or do I have to kick your butt?"

Ramon did not answer. He just stared at John as if John was a stranger. John had never displayed this kind of behavior before. Ramon heard a car driving up but he kept his eyes on John.

Tom's voice called out, "Dad, aren't you going to hit him?"

Another voice sliced through the tension. Jose spoke clearly and precisely. "Tom, stay out of this. You started the problem but let them work it out."

Tom ran at Jose, expecting to tackle him to the ground. Jose sidestepped and Tom went headfirst into a pile of chicken droppings. The chickens moved away from Tom but they laughed at the strange sight. "Serves him right for wanting to fight." They sputtered to each other.

"Now see what you've done?" Tom screamed.

John had seen enough. He said to Tom, "I want you to leave. Go home and get cleaned up. You're a mess."

John then faced Ramon and said, "I think you've caused enough trouble today. You can't order my son around like this place is yours. Go home and get your act together. You can't boss us around like you do people in other countries. You've worn out your welcome."

John got back in his car and started to back up. He did a double take as Yolanda emerge from the tool shed. "Who's that?" he asked Ramon.

"That's my daughter, Yolanda. Sometimes she helps me with the garden." Ramon hesitated for a few seconds. "But, since we're not welcome around here we'll pack up our things and go."

"Wait a minute, Ramon. I just returned from a long tiring trip. I may have been a little bit hasty. Give me a chance to apologize for my rude behavior. Perhaps you and your daughter could join me for dinner tonight. And yes, you can still use this area for your gardens."

John did not wait for a response. He said quickly, "I'll see you at seven." Then he smiled, backed out to the road and sped away.

Yolanda said, "Papa, thanks for keeping your temper under control. He's a jerk and there's no reason to associate with him anymore. I don't want to be around abusive people. I learned that lesson from Sergio. We're all together in this family. That's the way it should be."

THE FINAL GARDEN AND RAMON

Diminishing returns, negotiated settlements, and wars with the squirrels and rabbits worried Ramon throughout the fall and winter. He finally came up with a new strategy. Rather than continuing the fight he would join with Yolanda and Jose. Together they would grow a peace garden.

With the three of them working and sharing together they could produce more and enjoy the garden without wasting energy and time.

They chose an area that got plenty of sun but also got the afternoon shade. With a few hours of work they planned the garden and began preparing the soil. Yolanda and Jose left to prepare lunch.

Ramon stopped for just a moment to take a sip from his water bottle and put on his cap. He thought he could hear someone's voice but he dismissed the idea. No one was around. He would have seen any visitors coming up the road.

A small voice called out, "Whatcha doing, grandpa?" Ramon could not ignore the voice this time. Beside the shed a chubby brown rabbit smiled and waved. "I guess I should introduce myself. I'm Gabby. That's what my grandpa calls me but my real name is Gabriel. I like my name. Do you like it? Huh? Huh? Grandpa told me to check up on you. You haven't been looking very steady lately. You've fallen several times. Are you o.k.? Grandpa said you should be careful. He said maybe I should stick close to you just in case you need something.

Is that o.k. with you? I hope it is because I like being in the garden surrounded by vegetables."

Ramon couldn't have been sleeping because he just had water and was standing there leaning on his hoe. The rototiller was off to one side of the garden and the rows were finished, straight and neat. He must have done more than he thought and maybe that's why he was imagining this talkative rabbit.

He faced Gabby. "Get out of here! I don't want any critters in this garden. Go away!"

Gabby sniffed and said, "You hurt my feelings. Grandpa rabbit said you'd be grumpy at first. He worked with you last year but I think he should ignore you this year. I think he's being too patient. Why are you so grumpy? Are you always this way? Don't you like me? You don't need to get upset over everything. I'm just sayin…"

Ramon said loudly, "I'm going to put up an electric fence. That's what I'll do!"

"Suit yourself," Gabby muttered. "Uh, Grandpa, you might want to add some mulch, you know, grass clippings and leaves. This is a drought year and the mulch will help retain moisture. Grandpa rabbit said you were wise to put your garden close to the shed. Save fence material on one side, provide better drainage, and get more sun in the morning and shade in the afternoon. Most people don't think about that."

Gabby began walking the garden's perimeter while he chattered. "Throw in some mulch and this garden will get soft and mushy. You won't have as much trouble with the heavy clay. Last year when you watered you'd sink down in the clay and your shoes would get stuck. Then when you finally got out you had trouble getting it off your shoes. And when the clay dried it was like rock. Remember that, Grandpa? Jose and I didn't like to help in the garden because of that."

He paused and continued, "This isn't bad, Grandpa. The chicken manure will fertilize our plants and they will grow faster and start producing our vegetables sooner than we expected. Isn't that right, Grandpa?"

Ramon had been nodding in agreement, mesmerized by Gabby's endless words. Suddenly he came to life. "What do you mean, our vegetables! They're not yours at all!"

"You don't have to get so upset. I'll get some from my friend, Jose. He has his own garden and he'll share with me. I help him sometimes. Besides, I was just sayin.." Gabby ignored Ramon's hostile stare and continued. "The chickens that used to be here sure left a lot of manure. That's all chickens are good for. They don't do anything except lay an egg or two. A boy down the street claims rabbits can lay eggs, too. Right in the middle of spring some of the rabbits start laying colored eggs. I know because I've found some hidden in the tall grass and I've even some in bushes or trees. Some of the eggs are chocolate. Quite amazing, don't you think, Grandpa?

He lowered his voice as if he was sharing a secret. "So if rabbits can lay eggs, too, then there's no reason for chickens except for manure. They're not good to eat. Right, Grandpa?"

Ramon's answer did not come fast enough. Gabby eyed him suspiciously. "You don't eat chickens, do you?"

Caught off guard by Gabby's question, Ramon stared at the ground unsure how to answer without upsetting Gabby. Ramon looked up at the sky as if expecting angels to appear and rescue him. He couldn't lie.

"Yep. Chickens are one of our main food sources. If more people ate fruits and vegetables, maybe we wouldn't have to eat chicken."

Gabby said thoughtfully, "That's a shame about chickens. At least you don't eat rabbits. Right?"

Ramon knew no answer would satisfy Gabby so he waited quietly, knowing Gabby was ready to explode.

"That's cannibalism! That's terrible!" Gabby sputtered, horrified by the news. "I have to go see Grandpa rabbit. He never told me about this!"

Ramon watched Gabby sprint away and then he walked to the tool shed. He placed his hoe in a vise and sharpened one side of the hoe with a file and then turned the hoe over and sharpened the edge on the other side. "Who knows," he thought. "I might find a big toe in the garden someday. Wouldn't that be a surprise?"

He noticed how organized the tools were. Somebody had done a remarkable job putting everything in logical order. It was probably Yolanda or Jose. Ramon would have to thank them later.

Ramon planted his rows of tomatoes, peppers, zucchini, crooked neck, eggplants, onions, okra, green beans and corn. He planted as many varieties of each kind of plant he could. He enjoyed experimenting and he wanted something producing all the time.

He planted the rows closer together than he usually did. The drought this year was serious and he wanted to conserve water. He put in a drip system to water the bigger plants. He staked the tomatoes and put some in cages to support the weight of the vines and fruit. Finally, as a finishing touch, he put up poles just outside the garden and stretched three electric wires at various heights to dissuade visiting creatures. He plugged in his charger and flipped on the switch.

"Big critters. Little critters. Stay away," he roared. "You are not welcome here."

Over the last four months Ramon's balance had become a problem. When he bent to pick up something, he had to grab a pole or chair to straighten back up. In the garden there was nothing to grab and when he leaned over he had to be careful not to fall. Once he was down he discovered his strength was gone.

He had fallen a few times and he learned he could work his way up. He would lift up to being on his elbows, then his knees. After resting a few minutes he could stand up. The technique worked every time he accidently fell or deliberate moments when he got on his knees to gather low hanging tomatoes or other fruit.

Life continued at an almost normal pace. Every week he would gather his surplus vegetables and take them to the farmers' market. There were always customers and friends waiting for his arrival. "Hey, Farmer Garcia, what took you so long?" someone would ask. Then they would line up behind his truck until everything was gone. Then

Ramon would rush back to his garden and check what surprises he could bring to the next market.

His technique of pulling himself off the ground was sufficient until the day he forgot to turn off the water. The ground was drier and the temperature was hotter. The plants drooped and touched the ground. He pulled a hose to the garden so the thirsty plants could recover. "I'll let the water run about two hours," he thought. "That's all I need to get enough water to the plants." Then he went home and rested.

Four hours later Ramon woke up with an uneasy feeling that something was wrong. The thought would not go away. It nagged at him until he washed his hands. The running water reminded him of his unfinished task. "Oh, no!" he muttered as he rushed to the garden.

When he arrived he assessed the situation. Water was two inches deep in some spots and deeper in others. The water was still shooting out of the hose. The water had not spread as far as he feared but it was not being absorbed as well as he hoped. "Needed more mulch," he thought.

Ramon thought about going barefoot to avoid getting his shoes stuck in the mud but decided against it. There were too many stickers and his feet were tender. As he waded through the water he tripped over vines that had sprawled across the path. He recovered his balance each time. Then one shoe got stuck in the mud and he fell forward into a pool of water. At first he could not move but he rallied until he was on his knees. Although he was making progress the vines were still tangled around his ankles. He tugged and pulled but to no avail. The vines held fast.

Ramon unlaced one shoe and slipped it off. Then he took off the other shoe. Pulling himself free was still impossible. He stood but lost his balance and fell again. This time his face was in the water. He struggled but the mud clung to him and weighed him down. He crawled forward and was blocked by vines that seemed to be made of steel. He reversed his route and inched forward slowly. He thought he had found a way out until his head touched the electric fence. Zap! It was a small jolt but it got his attention. Twice more he bumped the fence and was jolted. Each time he recoiled in pain.

The water was providing an easy path for the electricity. The ground was snapping and popping around him as electricity pulsed through the electric fence. He tried to adjust his path accordingly to get away but by now the electricity had drained his strength.

It would be ridiculous to die in a few inches of water but he couldn't think of anything to do. No one could see him. There was no way to attract attention. For the moment he was stymied. He closed his eyes. Even though his face was in water there was nothing he could do but wait for the inevitable.

He thought he had died because the earth became alive. Then he dreamed he was flying high in the sky over trees and rivers. It was a strange feeling and he thought he saw the wings of angels flapping around him. The sensation was pleasant but short-lived. He was still exhausted from his previous efforts to escape the tomato patch. His muscles did not work. He couldn't move but the plants around him seemed to be in motion, swaying in waves as a large group of small animals passed through and then the plants were still.

After a few minutes Ramon realized he was on dry ground. He didn't remember the details but somehow he had escaped without the help of anyone else. As his strength returned, he decided he had to get up, get a hot meal, change into dry clothes, and go to the nearest clinic. He hated waiting but this time he would go and make sure he had no injuries, either internal or external. He reached out and grabbed a hoe that had mysteriously appeared and pulled himself to his knees. Using the hoe for balance he staggered to his feet.

There were many unanswered questions. No one could explain who called the ambulance, but it happened. No one could explain how Ramon got out of the water and onto dry ground. No one admitted turning off the electric fence and of course, the water. Who turned it off?

Ramon had a few days to think about these questions. He came up with answers but when he began telling his stories about the garden wars with rabbits and squirrels and other critters, people would just smile and walk away. He was considered delusional, on medication, and recovering from his accident. And there were some who thought Ramon was crazy.

The only ones who believed him were Yolanda, his daughter, and Jose, his grandson. Jose, the quiet boy who smiled a lot, knew when to be secretive. Jose's motto was this. 'If there was nothing to gain, why say anything?'

Although Jose had his own garden he enjoyed working in his grandpa's garden and watching things grow. Jose understood the relationship between earth and plants and animals. His grandpa had shown him how to plant, when to plant, and when to harvest the vegetables. Jose was a quick learner and he picked up techniques taught by the Aztecs as well as new discoveries from around the world.

Jose took the time to patiently explain everything he learned to Gabby. They worked side by side keeping Jose's garden in good repair. In addition, they secretly worked in Ramon's garden keeping tools organized and put away. Grandpa rabbit learned of their friendship and had approved it. The wars had ceased and the gardens were filled with ripening fruit.

Ramon, aka Grandpa Garcia, enjoyed giving away the garden's surplus to his neighbors, the hospital, and certain groups. But as he lay there on his bed he worried about all the vegetables and imagined them rotting on the vines.

Several times he threatened to get up and walk out of the hospital and get back to work. But when he mentioned the problem to Jose, his grandson smiled and said, "Grandpa, don't worry. We're taking care of the garden. We've got your back."

Ramon continued to worry though, until nurses and aides, technicians, volunteer workers, chaplains, secretaries, dietary and housekeeping personnel, and administrators stopped by to thank him for the delicious vegetables.

For several weeks every Monday and Thursday two five gallon buckets filled with tomatoes, peppers, eggplants, onions, zucchini, crooked neck squash, and assorted vegetables were left by Ramon's mailbox. At eight a.m. a physical therapist would stop, pick up the buckets, and deliver them to the hospital. At nine, two of the volunteer workers would take them to the volunteer station and put the vegetables on display. At the end of the second shift volunteers would return the empty buckets to a designated spot and someone would return the buckets to the garden.

Ramon never tired of hearing how his vegetables were appreciated. He would beam with pride. He was proud of his contributions and very proud of Jose.

Although Ramon was eager to return to his home there were complications. His doctor said, "Ramon, you've got pneumonia. You can't leave until we get it under control."

For the next two days Ramon planned a winter garden as he rested. He had time to think about his episode in the garden. He discussed it several times with Jose. Grandpa rabbit and Gabby were real. They and a large group of rabbits saved his life and he needed to thank them. He guessed he would have to discuss everything with Jose because no one else believed in talking rabbits, especially rabbits with compassion.

For three years Ramon had been on a mission to thwart rabbits and squirrels from decimating his vegetables. War had been declared and plants had been destroyed, but fortunately not one living critter had been harmed. The second year had been less stressful but hard feelings still existed. Ramon believed rabbits had taken control of his garden and he didn't like it.

He had grown up listening to stories of his Aztec ancestors, animals who changed the world, and tales of the unknown. It was ridiculous that it

took him so long to finally admit there were talking, organized rabbits. On the other hand, many of his aquaintences thought it was time for Farmer Garcia to see a psychiatrist. It was rumored that if he didn't watch out he would be declared incompetent. If it hadn't been for Jose, he might have turned himself in! Here he was, waving and talking to the air, rambling on about rabbits and squirrels. It made no sense to anyone listening. How could rabbits ruin this old man's life and then save him from drowning? And how could rabbits be angels and pick vegetables?

The people who overheard him were certain he had dementia or was overdosing on something. They thought he had lost his mind and because of that they avoided him.

Ramon knew he was old and weary but his mind was still sharp. He could still beat most people at checkers or dominoes. He read constantly and stayed current with the news. Yolanda was indignant that anyone would doubt his sanity. She talked to his doctor and with the doctor's help they convinced Ramon to take a two week vacation in Hawaii and let the talk die down.

When he was younger he had often traveled by plane with Yolanda from country to country. This trip, though, tired him out. Maybe it was the disease that tired him and not the plane. Over the last six months Ramon had noticed a gradual weakening of his arms and legs. Perhaps with rest and the right medications he could recover.

When the plane taxied down the runway Ramon felt a surge of excitement. He must grab his luggage before anyone noticed.

"Where do we pick up our luggage," he asked Jose. "I need to get it quickly."

"Don't worry, Grandpa," Jose said quietly. "They'll be all right."

They watched their luggage bounce as a luggage handler hurried to get their suitcases on a cart. Ramon pressed against a window, trying to tell the handler to take it easy.

Jose grabbed his arm. "Grandpa, don't let them know Grandpa rabbit is here."

Ramon heeded the warning. His grandson was right. There would have been trouble if a rabbit was found. He had promised there would be no trouble. He swallowed his pride and said nothing.

Later, as Ramon and Grandpa rabbit sat on their lounge chairs sipping their second pina coladas, Ramon said, "Louis, this is the life. No worries or work. Just sit in the shade and relax all day."

Louis chuckled, "If only there were a few beach bunnies with a volley ball. Then it would be perfect."

In the distance someone began singing and people began cheering. A voice boomed from speakers, "we are fortunate to have with us this afternoon a young singer with an outstanding voice. Give it up for Don Jose, the guy who sang "Tiny Bubbles," last summer in our talent contest. This year he's added a new twist, a mariachi band combined with music of Hawaii! It's strange but very unique. It's delightful!"

The young man strummed his guitar and then sang with confidence. His voice grew louder and stronger and the crowd grew quiet. After the first song there was thunderous applause. He sang another song and then another before the crowd began chanting, "Don, Don, Don, Don, Don. Sing your song." And then, "Canta para nosotros." He sang Tiny Bubbles twice, once in English and once in Spanish. The crowd went wild.

Don Jose raised both arms in triumph. He spun around on his heels and waved to the three figures reclining on the beach. Grandpa Rabbit, Yolanda, and Ramon waved back.

Then Don Jose turned to the crowd. "To peace and love. This song is dedicated to those who tirelessly work to restore peaace among all groups, including people and animals!" The crowd applauded and stood up. When the noise subsided, Don Jose sang out 'Tiny Bubbles……'.

Grandpa rabbit and Grandpa Garcia looked at each other and laughed. "Our grandsons turned out all right,' Grandpa Garcia said. "We couldn't have done any better."

Gabby's voice boomed, "Grandpa, are you ready for another juice? Maybe a carrot juice this time?" he waited for an answer but hearing none he asked, "Grandpa Garcia, do you need anything?" There was silence. Gabby walked over and checked each recliner."Yep," he chuckled. Both were sleeping peacefully. He didn't want to wake them up. He laughed and said quietly, "This is going to be a fun summer."

The end of the story should have stopped there but Ramon discovered once again that life goes on. When they returned from their trip to Hawaii, everything seemed normal at first. But gradually Ramon discovered things had been moved, changed, and adjusted. He asked the spirits if someone had been in his house. The spirits answered with a resounding yes. Once Ramon opened the pathway the spirits were eager to help.

Someone had set small cameras and listening devices throughout the house. It was evident that the intruder did not expect anyone to find them. Whoever it was, he or she was highly skilled. The spirits showed him all ten and how to dismantle them without being obvious. But questions remained. What was taken? What were they looking for?

Ramon, Jose, and Yolanda could not determine if anything was missing. There was no tape to replay. Everything was fed to remote cameras.

Ramon knew Yolanda was a specific target. She had questioned her husband in front of others, and worse yet, she had gotten away from his two best men. He could not rest until she was eliminated. Ramon and Jose were witnesses and therefore marked as victims. Daniel and Ana were the children he wanted. They could be trained but Yolanda could never have them.

There were rumors about Sergio and his connections to the drug world. Ramon heard stories about Sergio's cruelties and his rise in power. There were those who insisted Sergio drove a silent motorcycle, coming into town on the wind. Others reported that he appeared as a movie star, arriving in a long limo, eating at a local restaurant, discussing news of Yolanda and his three children, and then leaving town without trying to contact any of them.

Jose, his oldest, had always had problems in school. Sergio considered Jose to be a loser with no thinking skills or talents. Sergio paid no attention to news stories about a young singer who was beginning to draw crowds with his songs in several languages. Sergio also ignored the reports that Jose was enrolled in college taking courses in Mechanical Engineering. Sergio simply pretended Jose was not his son.

He was curious about his two younger children, Daniel and Maria. There was a chance they could learn how to run his business. He wanted someone he could trust and family connections were better than friends. When Daniel and Maria were older, he would train them properly.

It was early summer. The garden was growing but no fruit was ripe. Ramon wanted to take his three grandchildren on a short trip somewhere beautiful. He asked Yolanda to name a place she had always wanted to visit.

She thought for a moment. "I've always wanted to visit Yosemite. I've seen pictures of the granite mountains, the waterfalls, and the tall redwoods. I've heard the views are spectacular. People from all over the world make special trips there. We live so close and yet we haven't seen the beauty in our own back yard."

Ramon was pleased with her selection. Yosemite was a garden created by god and the spirits when the world began. His three grandchildren should see the beauty for themselves. It was something they would remember for the rest of their lives.

He managed to rent one of the housekeeping units online. Then he carefully researched what they might need for camping. He began his list with sleeping bags, foam pads, cooking utensils, personal items like tooth paste. He decided they would enjoy their experience more if they gathered their own supplies.

He insisted they discuss the items on his list and add or subtract items if the whole group agreed on what was necessary. Some items were removed and replaced by items Ramon thought were a luxury. He packed and repacked their camping supplies. Ramon checked his list one last time for changes.

The day before they left, Ramon and Jose began packing the car. Each family member got to add one item if it fit without disruption of the process. Ramon packed a bottle of maple syrup. Jose chose his guitar. Yolanda. Books to read. Daniel and Maria chose ipads with their favorite games. Everybody was happy.

The trip was longer than expected, the road more winding, the car more crowded. When they arrived all were tired and grumpy. Instead of cooking that first evening they decided to eat pizza, bought from a pizza kiosk, take showers and go right to bed. The only exception was the story of "The Big Toe", told by Ramon as they gathered around the fire. Within minutes they were all sound asleep.

The crisp clear silence was interrupted by metal slamming against metal. Wham! Bam! Ramon knew what was causing the racket. A bear was outside their tent, checking their food supplies. The bear grunted as it shuffled around the camp site. The bear stopped, sniffed three times and then once more, realizing it had located a rare treasure.

Ramon felt his stomach tightening. "That bear discovered my expensive maple syrup. I was going to pour it over my pancakes for breakfast. Maybe the bear will get discouraged and go away."

Daniel woke up and grabbed Jose's arm. He shook it. "Jose, Jose! There's a bear outside and it's getting into our food! I thought the locker was supposed to keep out bears!"

Ramon put his head back down. "Be very quiet. If we don't disturb it the bear should leave soon. It's hungry and after food. The food locker must be broken."

At the camp meeting the rangers had insisted the lockers were strong enough and complex enough that bears could not break in. The ranger in charge told all the campers that the animals could be dangerous but only when confronted by a human. He marked spots on a map where encounters had taken place over the last five weeks. When the rangers left, Ramon said quietly, "Some of the bears are very dangerous. Others are not. We will have to stay away from all of them until we know for sure."

Wham! Bam! This was getting irritating.

"Jose and Daniel, stay where you are," Yolanda whispered. "Remember what the ranger said today. Stay away from wild animals, especially the bears! They won't hurt anyone if they are left alone!"

Ramon sat up. Something was wrong. Where was Ana?

"Yolanda, where is Ana?"

The two boys raised their heads wearily. "What's going on?"

Then they began to realize that Ramon was serious. "Mama, where's Ana?" they said together.

Ramon glanced around. Even though he was old and slow he was the man in charge. "I'll look outside. Don't worry, Yolanda. I'll find her."

He didn't wait for a response. Quickly he pulled on his shorts and slipped on his shoes. He was trying to hurry but Jose and Daniel were on their way out. They didn't get very far before they saw her.

They stopped suddenly and melted into the darkness, fascinated by the scene in front of them. Ana sat a few feet from the bear, chatting away as if the bear was a long lost friend. He was listening intently as she chatted. He cocked his head one way and then the other.

Ramon decided Ana was not in any danger. As she sat there Ramon was reminded of Yolanda as a little girl and their trips to the zoo. Yolanda had never been afraid of any of the animals. Ramon smiled. Ana had the blood of her ancestors flowing through her veins. She wasn't afraid. She had taken charge of the situation and was playing school. The bear grunted and shifted his weight but he didn't dare move. Ana would have been mad. In fact, she was pretending to be his teacher.

The bear nodded and grinned as Ana answered his questions. She explained how bees made honey. She told him about the famous Teddy Bear and about Pooh bear. Then the bear rocked back and looked up as she pointed out Ursa Major and Ursa Minor. The bear was delighted. No one had taken the time to teach him before.

Ramon coughed. He didn't mean to cough but his throat was dry. The sound got the bear's attention and his head snapped around. His eyes were small and red, saliva dripped from his teeth, and he tensed, ready to roar and pounce upon this intruder.

Ana laughed. "Don't be such a mean looking bear. That's just my brothers and my Grandpa Ramon. He always checks up on me to make sure I'm safe."

Ramon stepped closer, not yet sure where the imaginary boundaries were that separated them. Without talking, the bear communicated with them. "Three times a day during the summer I have to practice looking ferocious. When campers see me I roar and threaten. They are scared, jump in their cars or rv's, and I get to eat the scattered food. If things go well and people tell their stories to others, the crowds grow and I get bonus food, some for now and some for winter supplies. It works out well."

"Ana has been such fun. I usually don't have a chance to relax but she put me at ease right away. I've got to run. The early bird campers cause a lot of problems. They go to the river very early to fish or meditate. I have to be gone before they get there. "Glad to meet you, Ramon. Thanks, Ana, for everything."

The huge bear glanced over his shoulder and disappeared into the brush.

Ramon said, "We'd better get back inside before someone claims the bear was ready to attack us."

As they crawled back into their sleeping bags Yolanda said, "I was worried at first but the spirits assured me all of you were o.k. There were others who saw you and you might have to explain why you were in harm's way. Ramon, you'll probably be blamed for not protecting Ana."

Yolanda was right. Rumors were rampant. Right after daybreak men began arriving, bringing their horses in trailers, getting ready to hunt the bear that waited around campgrounds and attacked unsuspecting victims.

Ramon told the mounted posse the bear had wandered into camp, and when it saw Ramon and his family, it fled in terror. The posse listened but did not seem convinced that Ramon was telling the truth.

The group found no evidence the bear was trying to harm people, so they left but not without warning Ramon, "Bears and people are not meant to be together. If you encourage encounters with wild animals you could be fined or banned from national parks. Stay out of trouble."

That night Ramon had a nightmare about the bear. In his dream his father was yelling at him. "Ramon, how many times must I tell you? One of your jobs is to protect your sister! You failed again. Be a man. Follow orders!"

He turned and said, "Stay away from publicity. Ramon, I don't want to read about you getting into trouble."

In his journals Ramon never mentioned that Sergio and his father were both bullies. His dad was dead and there was no point in insulting his name. Ramon did not want to bring fear into their lives either. Recently Sergio had been seen around town, asking questions about Daniel and Ana. Ramon was worried. Sergio and his men would try to hurt someone. Ramon had no doubt about that.

After they returned from Yosemite, they inspected the house again. Just by looking there was no evidence anyone had been there. But according to the spirits, four people had checked each room.

That night Ramon went from room to room checking locks and checking each monitoring device. Somebody had replaced the devices taken earlier. The new ones were smaller and harder to find. Ramon asked the spirits to help him find them. Anyone intending harm should not have an advantage.

He wanted to leave at 5 a.m. and take the kids somewhere they could be safe. A light rain was falling and the streets would be slippery. The first rain of the season brought the oils up from the asphault and warning signs would be everywhere. All the lights were off and he wandered about the house carefully lifting his feet. This would be a terrible time to fall.

Everyone was sleeping. They were tired but happy after their trip. Yosemite had been more beautiful than he remembered. They would have to go in the spring when the snows were melting, the waterfalls were cascading down the granite, the giant sequoias were green and clean, the animals were coming out of hibernation or had newborns, and the crowds of people were walking or bicycling everywhere.

Ramon heard a slight sound near the front window. Then breaking glass. The window was opening slowly. Ramon could see shapes and shadows waiting outside. Someone would come through the window and let the others in.

He thought about his gun but that was not a good idea. He might shoot two but he couldn't stop them all. He could call the police but they would get there too late. When they arrived a gun battle in the dark might get one of his loved ones hurt or killed.

Ramon woke Yolanda first and then Jose. "Time to see if the spirits can help us," he whispered.

The front door opened and Ramon could hear feet padding across the carpet. He was in the hallway when an Aztec warrior raced by heading for the group of intruders. Shots were fired. Ramon ducked into a room.

"I think I got him," a voice called out. "I couldn't miss at that range."

Two more warriors carrying spears and shields ran past Ramon. They pushed him into his room. "We don't need your help right now. Keep safe."

Ramon heard more shots, a thud as a body hit the floor, and then silence.

Footsteps getting closer, as three people stumbled towards him. Behind them two warriors screamed war cries, and it was enough to make them the three people stop and turn around. Jose stepped out of his room and swung a chair. The first man was caught by surprise as the chair crashed into him. He dropped to the ground. Ramon hit the second man across the throat with his cane. The man grabbed his throat and he also fell to the floor.

The third man, raised a gun. "Two of you are going to be dead," he said. He tried to pull the trigger but he couldn't. The gun's barrel lifted and turned. He fought to bring it forward again. The barrel turned and pointed at his forehead.

Daniel and Ana stepped out of their rooms. Both of them were staring intently at the man. "You are a bad man. You wanted to hurt us."

The man placed the barrel against his head. "Don't shoot. Please don't shoot." Even though he held the gun, he did not control the gun.

With duct tape the three men were securely tied, each separately, and without a chance to escape. The warriors watched from the walls.

"Where is Sergio?" Ramon asked.

"He stayed in the car. He's waiting until we give him the signal that Yolanda, Ramon, and Jose are dead."

They looked outside at the empty car. "Where is he?" Jose asked.

One of the warriors said, "He's got a gas can and he's going to burn this house down with you in it."

Yolanda stepped outside. She saw Sergio pouring gas across the front porch. "Sergio, you can't burn our bodies because none of us are dead."

Sergio's face was contorted with rage. He lifted the gas can over his head and positioned his feet. He was ready to throw it at Yolanda.

"Control yourself, Sergio," Yolanda said. "I'm not afraid of you anymore.

One bad move will put you in danger."

Sergio did not listen. He threw the can. The can traveled two feet before it hit an invisible wall.

Gas splashed all over him.

"Don't move, Sergio. We will get you out if you relax."

Sergio pulled out a gun. "You can't tell me what to do. You've been worthless to me. Give me the kids and I'll go."

"No. Sergio. You're all alone. You get nothing except a chance to live."

Sergio tried to lift his gun but his arms would not move. "Get off of me! Let me go! You can't do this to me!"

Ramon said, "I hear sirens. Sergio, I think you should put your gun away."

Sergio and his gang were convicted of various crimes and were sentenced to ten years in prison. With the help of certain politicians they were granted a new trial due to irregularities regarding jury conduct. After three short years they were released despite the objections of various law enforcement officials, prosecuting attorneys, and victims.

Ramon did not worry about their early release despite the jubilations in the underworld. He privately told those who were upset and angry, that Sergio and his gang would now answer to a higher court. Ramon's friends shook their heads in confusion. Ramon had finally lost all reason.

Ramon looked around at the gardens. Everything was quiet and peaceful. Jose, Yolanda, Daniel, and Ana were helping the rabbits with their garden of plenty. Sergio and his group were raking and hoeing alongside Aztec warriors in their garden of peace. There would be no struggles for power or wealth at the expense of others for as long as Ramon wanted. Sergio might escape in a world of reality but in the spirit world he was captured forever. Justice would be served.

Ramon was no longer depressed. He no longer felt trapped, forgotten, and devalued. His worlds had blended. Fantasy and reality were one and the same.

He closed his journal. How could he explain his life to others? He smiled and waved at Gabby. There was no need to explain. Life was what he made it to be. Perfect.

Printed in the United States
By Bookmasters